Roche Harbor Caper

By

D. M. Ulmer

Tea and Crumpet Capers

Patriot Media, Inc. is proud to introduce our newest line of titles, featuring upscale and sophisticated, light stories in the mystery/suspense/thriller genre written by our Patriot Media Authors.

Enjoy the *first* novel in the Michael Kincaid series

Missing Person

By W.H. Hesse & D.M. Ulmer

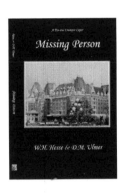

Retired Marine Corps Sergeant Major Kincaid, turned Associate Professor of English literature, moonlights as a writer of mystery novels. He is approached by a woman *fan* who misconstrues his literary talent for bona fide detecting skills. She retains him to locate her son with whom she has lost contact for twenty years. Kincaid reluctantly accepts and finds himself in a quagmire of intrigue, greed, and murder. The drama is set in and around Port Angeles, near Washington State's magnificent Olympic Mountains.

The *third* novel in the Michael Kincaid series:
The Long Beach Caper by D.M. Ulmer

Michael Kincaid, a retired Marine Corps Sgt. Major turned English Literature Professor, and his wife Doris, become involved in a caper while on their honeymoon in Long Beach, WA. Their first day at Long Beach, a stranger recognizes Michael as the author of the Harry Steele detective novel series, introduces himself, then asks Michael to investigate a mundane problem within his family, keeping or disposing of their three generation legacy; the Heinrich Voelcker farm in Idaho.

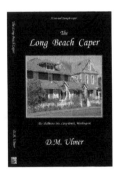

The Roche Harbor Caper

By D.M. Ulmer

Second Edition
Copyright © 2010 by D.M. Ulmer
All rights reserved.

Second Edition
ISBN-13: 978-0-9845777-1-2
Original Manuscript – D.M. Ulmer
Technical Review Editor – Nelson O. Ottenhausen
Sr. Editor – Doris Littlefield
Cover Photos – D.M. Ulmer
Second Edition Cover Layout – Dari Bradley

This is a fictional story: Use or mention of historical events, places, names of anyone or any similarity of the story line to actual persons, places or events is purely coincidental.

Published by Patriot Media, Incorporated
Publishing America's Patriots
P.O. Box 5414
Niceville, FL 32578
United States of America
www.patriotmediainc.com

Dedication

For my wife, Carol, whose constant love and support made this work possible.

Acknowledgements

Las Plumas, a literary critique group which meets regularly in facilities of the King County, Washington Library System, provided invaluable counsel with this effort. Dave Bartholomew, Dagmar Braun-Jones, Barbara Brown, June Goehler, Barbara Boyle, Margie Hussey, Wayne and Doris Littlefield, Doris a superb syntax and line editor, Liz McCord, Sue Meyers, Gina Simpson, Jan and Scott Stahr, and Kornelia Whitmore.

Prologue

Thomas Hawke looked up from behind his desk aboard the palatial yacht *Vega* then tried to contain his emotions; his eyes bulged while blood vessels threatened to burst through his forehead as he shouted, "Not a dime! Not one red cent, Frederick!"

Frederick, his son, stood before him in the repentant posture Thomas had seen far too often. "But Father, I'm sorry. This won't happen again, ever."

Frederick's shoulders shook in what Thomas surmised to be feigned sobbing, another common ruse of his ne'er-do-well, sole heir.

"No more bailouts, Frederick. These do not work and they only enable your failures. Lord knows there is an abundance of those."

Anger slowly replaced the humility as he asked, "But what will I do, Father?"

"Go out and find yourself a job. You've got a degree, family connections. Most people do much more with considerably less. It's time to try your wings, and get out of this one on your own, Frederick." Thomas's voice reverted to the tones of a father encouraging his son to succeed. "For the first time, do something to make you feel good about yourself."

Frederick pleaded, "But why not the next time?"

Frustration returned to Thomas's voice. "You've answered your own question. Already, you concede there will be a next time and preordain your own failure. All I have will be yours someday, but this is not a given. First, you must show me you can do more than squander away the fortune I have worked so hard for. You seem unable to realize a fortune without personal pride is like an empty glass."

Thomas knew how much his son hated one of those.

"Can we talk about this in the morning?"

"No, Frederick. We've already gone through too many *in the morning* discussions. Leave for Seattle and start looking. Your apartment is paid through August, and I'll continue a modest allowance. But first, get yourself into Gamblers Anonymous. You're a sick man, Frederick. Until cured, your life will be miserable. Believe me."

"That's your final word, Father?"

"My final word."

Frederick turned on his heel and stomped out of the study, slamming the door behind him.

Clarissa Hawke, Thomas's wife, awakened with a start. She heard a loud splash through the *Vega's* hull. *Had someone fallen overboard?* The digital clock in her bedroom read 2:00 a.m. A short time later the sound of a small outboard engine could be heard.

She considered it to be someone in the marina setting out for an early check of their crab pots, part of the attraction that brings so many boaters to Roche Harbor in the summer. *Surely, everything must be well,* she thought.

Clarissa fell back into a deep sleep.

Miguel Vargas, Crew Chief of the *Vega,* awoke to the sound of a light thumping against the hull. He and his wife, Isabel, occupied a cabin at the waterline.

He sat up in his bunk, enjoyed a good stretch then quietly arose so as not to disturb his wife, a gentle and loving woman, except when roused from a sound sleep. He silenced the alarm a few minutes before it would have gone off at 5:00 a.m.

Miguel must awaken his crew, but first get two pots of coffee going in the galley, one for his men, and the other, a special Colombian blend for his boss, the early rising Thomas Hawke. Then Miguel would go topside and check out the source of the noise that had awakened him. He bowed to the portrait of Our Lady of Guadalupe and crossed himself.

An errant deadhead likely thumped against *Vega's* hull, a log so water soaked it barely floated. Many of these drift throughout the waters in and adjacent to Puget Sound. Ten minutes later, the coffee started, he went topside to savor the serenity and quiet of early morning. How he loved this position he and Isabel had secured.

Walking to the rail near where he had heard the thumping sound, Miguel looked over the side and into the lifeless face of Thomas Hawke. "Madre Dios!"

Miguel gave the alarm and all aboard *Vega* assembled on the main deck—all except Frederick Hawke.

The Roche Harbor Caper

Chapter 1

Professor Michael Kincaid addressed his class at the final session before end of term at the University of Washington, Port Angeles campus. He preferred standing, rather than speak from the seat at his desk. A retired Sergeant Major of the U.S. Marine Corps, traits he developed as a drill instructor had been too well ingrained for it to be otherwise. His six-two frame, imposing, if not intimidating accommodated his belief there could be no learning without discipline.

With his eyes flashing his typical challenge, Michael asked, "So what have you got to show for all your parents' tuition money from English Literature I?"

Michael's middle fifties slipped too quickly into memory.

The students liked him and they became comfortable in his classroom almost immediately. His policy, there are no dumb questions or comments—only dumb rejoinders.

June Morales, student with best prospects of becoming a writer herself, did not surprise Michael by being first to raise her hand. "Professor Kincaid, you always ask us when we finish a piece, 'What do you believe the writer is trying to say?' If a person is capable only of trying to say something then they can't be a very accomplished writer."

Eyes of the class turned to Michael with anticipation. The duels between June and their professor frequently provided a source of entertainment. This time hopes of his taking the opposite view went quickly up in smoke.

June's IQ being well off the scale permitted her to see through a fog job like a recently washed window. Michael measured his response carefully. "Maybe I owe the class an apology. I think the only reason I've asked that question is because that's what my Profs always asked me." June's face fell in disappointment. She wanted to tilt with Michael a final time and worked hard to ready herself. She did not expect him to agree with her. She took the safe ground.

"Would you expand, please?"

"Herman Melville was an American author, so not covered in this course. I seriously doubt his Moby Dick was anything more than a sea adventure intended to entertain its readers. Melville was far too good a writer to embed his message in a work of fiction and expect his readers to discover it. Consider the popularly accepted allegory: *good triumphs over evil*. This is preaching to the choir for nineteenth century readers."

He had to let June off the hook. "Good question, Ms. Morales. Despite my involvement on the apparent other side of the equation during the sixties, I consider the greatest slogan to emerge from the anti-war movement to be, *question authority*. I count on you guys to do that, but respectfully. When someone else's opinion doesn't track with yours, give that person the benefit of the doubt. *Argumentum ad hominem* - it means to attack the proponents/opponents of an issue rather than dealing with the issue on its own merits. It's likely his best effort to work the problem. Husband your energies accordingly. Challenge issues—not the people. Nice going, Ms. Morales."

What began as mild applause ended with each student beating his hands together vigorously then climbing atop their chairs and continuing to applaud. This bowled Michael over.

Well damn it, maybe I finally did something right.

Another student asked, "So what was Harry Steele trying to say in *Broken Pendant?*"

Michael countered, "Why don't you ask Harry Steele?"

He knew his nom de plume for the popular detective novel series to be common knowledge about the campus.

"Now, if that's the most on your minds, good-bye, congratulations, and it has been my pleasure to have you in my class. Dismissed!"

Michael glanced at his watch. In fifty minutes, a Kenmore Air floatplane would deliver his son, Second Lieutenant Joseph Unger, USMC, to Sequim. Joseph would join Michael and Doris Baker there for a weekend 'getting to know you' sail to Roche Harbor in the San Juan Islands, across the Strait of Juan de Fuca.

Everyone knew of his interest in Dean Benson's secretary except Michael.

Doris Baker sat on the fantail of *Vietvet*, a 1958 model Blanchard wooden hull racing sailboat, moored at John Wayne Marina, Sequim. Michael's friend, Deputy Sheriff Jim Epsom, a gifted woodworker, had literally salvaged the classy lady from a scrap heap and converted her into a thing of beauty. *Vietvet* had provided Michael's temporary quarters while he underwent application for employment at the college. It pleased Epsom to do this for his comrade with whom he had shared many harrowing times during the Vietnam conflict.

Vietvet sported a white hull with blue trim, and featured a handsomely varnished mast that rose fifty-eight feet above her sleek, thirty-eight foot hull, highest in the marina. An aluminum mast would have made more sense and required far less maintenance, but in the words of Jim Epsom, "Wood looks so damn much better." So each winter, he painstakingly lowered it to repair the ultraviolet ray damage done the previous summer. After many sails together, Jim had declared his friend qualified to solo and frequently made a loan of it to Michael, itself a statement of his great confidence in Kincaid.

Doris chatted with her twenty-six-year-old daughter, Elizabeth, who pursued a masters in speech communication at the University of Washington in Seattle. Liz, as her mom chose to call her, hoped to find her way into sports media, natural for her, being an accomplished athlete. She had excelled in volleyball and track. Liz arrived on the scene unexpectedly this weekend, unaware of Doris's impending sea voyage with Michael and his son.

"No problem, Mom!" Liz declared. "I'll hang out at your place. I got a backlog of summer reading you wouldn't believe." Liz had driven her mom to the marina. "Okay to stick around and meet your new boyfriend?"

"He is not my boyfriend," Doris said in the stern voice used traditionally to tell her daughter *that's that.* It had never worked before and not expected to work now.

Liz looked back at her mom and took a pull from a cold Corona. A slice of lime floated in the bottle. "C'mon, Mom. Just like you always used to tell me. 'We can share anything.' That was when you wanted to know what I was up to. It's payback time!"

Doris looked at her watch. It fast approached 2:00 p.m. "If we don't get moving we won't make it to Roche by nightfall."

"Nice try, Mom. What's the straight poop on Michael?" Liz twirled a strand of shoulder length hair. Once a towhead, she had become a muddy blonde.

Doris Baker wished her daughter to be more serious about her grooming, but Liz remained a free spirit.

"You know, you could come with us. There's plenty of room on this thing." Jim Epsom would have blanched on hearing his pride and joy referred to as a *thing.*

"Not in your wildest dreams! This is your kid who lives in the big city. My camping out days are over. Matter of fact, they never began. And don't think I'm not getting my answer." Liz put the train back on the tracks. "Give up, Mom. You know what a pest I can be!" Liz appeared comfortable in white shorts and blue tank top. Long legs rested comfortably in a bright sun on the sailboat transom, as a pair of cornflower blue eyes bore in on her mom.

"He's a very nice man, and we're good friends. Michael is an excellent professor, a favorite of Dean Benson."

"He put any moves on you?"

"Liz! We've only known each other a coupla months!"

"So, no sleepovers or hanky-panky on the sailboat?"

Doris shook her head. She loved her daughter's unaffected candor. "We belong to different generations."

"It's the mid-nineties for you too. And you look great, Mom. You notice I don't introduce you to any of my hot guys."

Michael Kincaid's appearance spared Doris from further bombardment by her daughter. Michael walked down the dock beside his son, Second Lieutenant Joseph Unger, tall like his dad and cutting a trim figure in his Marine Corps summer khaki uniform.

While still out of earshot, Liz said to her mom, "OH MY GOD!"

Doris had already met Joseph, so introductions to only Liz needed to me made.

After the exchange of handshakes, Liz said, "Mom says I can come along, Professor Kincaid. Can you wait till I run up to the car and get my bag?"

A gentle westerly wind, ten knots by Joseph's reckoning paralleled the Strait and *Vietvet* moved on a beam reach heading directly for Roche Harbor. Perfect weather permitted the dodger to be folded down.

"Let me drive, Joe," Liz pleaded. He actually preferred the shortened version of his name, the full Joseph a concession to his dad and Doris Baker.

"You mean steer, Liz. If you're going to be a seaman, you gotta use the right phraseology."

"Whatever." Liz had survived her initial shock and had reassumed her blasé attitude. The inventive Jim Epsom had removed the original tiller and replaced it with a stainless steel helm. He made only this concession to available technological improvement. Built in 1958, the charm of sailing *Vietvet* centered on operating her with original equipment. Even the ship to shore radio hashed its original squeaky voice in the cabin, though Jim had a modern one kept in a locker in the event of emergency.

"Okay, Liz, you got it," said Joe and he stepped aside.

"Which way do I go?"

"By the compass, we're heading zero one nine." He gestured toward the binnacle stand.

"I see," she said. "What are those round things on each side of the compass?"

"The compass tries to follow the earth's magnetic lines of force, but the boat's magnetic field interrupts that. They're called quadrantal spheres, and they correct for the boat's magnetism." He didn't know her well enough to use the common nickname: navigator's balls.

"Liz, it's tough to steer by the compass when you're just starting out. See that island ahead of us?"

"That one?" she replied, pointing in the direction of San Juan Island.

"Yep. Steer just like you would a car, and keep us headed to the extreme left side of the island." Joe didn't need a telltale to measure the direction and force of the relative wind. Liz's ponytail performed that function quite well. He watched her long enough to see her intelligence and natural athletic ability enabled her to easily perform this task.

"So, you learned how to do this at Annapolis?" Liz asked. "I thought you were studying to be a Marine."

Joe stole admiring glances at her. "We got exposed to just about everything. They have a few yawls there, boats about the size of this, so we had to learn how to sail them."

"Oh? Well tell me Mr. Sailboat man, how can we sail across the Strait with the wind blowing in the wrong direction? I thought the wind had to be behind us."

Joe gestured upward. The wooden mast groaned slightly in response to wind pressure; white sails, in contrast to the royal blue sky, billowed magnificently like a pair of angel wings. "We're like a big kite on its side. With the wind at your back, the kite goes up, right? Put it on its side, and it goes sideways.

See? The wind is blowing directly on our portside, the west, so we're able to kite to the north."

She didn't understand, but conceded Joseph the point on the strength of how convincing he sounded. "How long for us to get to ... where are we going?"

"Roche Harbor in the San Juans."

Liz, not famous for her patience, asked, "Well, how long will that take?" She noticed Joe's sandy hair and guessed it to be curly, but could not tell with his military cut.

"Depends on how fast we go." Joe enjoyed Liz's curiosity, however short-lived.

"Well, how fast are we going?" Liz grew impatient. She'd grown accustomed to men anticipating her needs.

Joe contemplated her through green eyes and a smile. He beheld Liz's delicate and well-defined features. *Damn pretty,* he thought. "My guess is about six knots."

"Knots?"

"Work with me, Liz. On the water, we say knots for speed."

"So how do you know we're going six knots?"

"Just a guess. We can measure it if you like?"

"We got a speedom ... knotometer?"

"No. Here." He picked up a dilapidated tennis ball from the transom. "Take this all the way to the bow and drop it over the side." He took over the helm.

"Bow?"

"Yeah, the pointy end. Be careful not to fall over the side."

Liz looked at him through an expression that said, 'Don't you know I'm an athlete?' As she walked past her mom, stretched in a deck chair beside Michael, Liz rolled her eyes.

"Having that much fun?" Doris asked.

"Actually, I'm learning a lot." Liz had no wish to criticize Joe in the presence of his father.

"He must take after his dad," Doris said to her daughter.

Michael whispered quietly to Doris. "When Joseph gets going, he can drive you up a tree."

Liz reached *Vietvet's* bow. "Okay, Joe!"

"Okay," he shouted.

Liz dropped the ball and Joe started his stopwatch as Liz made her way back to the helm.

"So, how fast are we going?"

"Here, take the wheel," Joe said. He broke out a small notebook and performed several calculations. "We're making six and a half knots," Joe announced, pride obvious in his voice.

"How do you know that?" Liz began to wonder if Joe yanked her around.

"The boat's thirty-eight feet long, right?"

"If you say so."

"It took three and a half seconds for the ball to go from bow to stern, thirty-eight feet. A ship making six and a half knots goes thirty-eight feet in three point five seconds."

He looked at Liz for a sign of admiration and found none. "San Juan Island looks to be about five miles away. We should be at the harbor in fifty minutes, or so."

Liz decided she would ask no more questions.

Taking Jim Epsom's advice, Michael elected the northern approach to Roche Harbor. The shorter, but tortuous back channel deemed it better for a first timer to make that passage with someone who has been there and done that.

Michael turned up the gain to *Vietvet's* scratchy ship to shore radio and clicked the press-to-talk button several times. It seemed to be working.

"Roche, this is *Vietvet*, two miles north with a reserved berth."

"Roger, *Vietvet*. Continue. Your berth is northwest of I dock. Turn in just before the yacht *Vega*. She's big. Doubt you'll miss her."

"Copy, Roche. *Vietvet* out," Michael said in a crisp monotone.

Joseph fired up the diesel and then assisted his dad to douse and bag the sails. They would enter port *shipshape and Bristol fashion*, the manner established by owner Jim Epsom.

"Guess they won't let us bring her in on the rags?" Joseph asked his dad. He referred to sailing all the way to the dock, a maneuver demanding far greater skills than those possessed by Michael.

"Even we're not that good, and we don't want to embarrass ourselves in front of the ladies."

"Speak for yourself, Dad." His son grinned at Michael.

Vietvet entered the harbor and made her way past G and H docks. One hundred forty-eight feet of the palatial yacht *Vega* lay moored at the end of I dock.

Liz's comment for the second time that day: "Oh my God!"

Michael nodded to his son and said in a low voice, "Life is good, Joseph. Why do the poor complain so much?"

Vietvet maneuvered smoothly into her slip. On the dock, a Hispanic man directed the efforts of several line handlers.

"Be quick about it!" shouted a man in his middle thirties, nattily attired in white slacks, blue blazer and cap with gold braid on the bill. The Hispanic man gave his boss a scowl and went about his work. The gold braid said, "Beautiful boat, skipper."

Michael knew he didn't deserve the credit but replied his thanks anyway.

With *Vietvet* safely moored, Michael walked onto the dock to thank the gold braid.

"Welcome to Roche! The cocktail flag is flying aboard *Vega*. Won't you join my guests and me? I'm Frederick Hawke."

Chapter 2

With an uncharacteristic edge to her voice, Doris asked, "Do you know who that was?"

Michael replied, "Should I?"

"Frederick Hawke's father died here at Roche three years ago under mysterious circumstances. For a time, Frederick had been the prime suspect, but the San Juan County Sheriff's office cleared him."

"This is supposed to be a holiday. What's with the mysterious bit?"

"I thought Harry Steele didn't take holidays," Doris added.

"I'm gonna hear about this whether I want to or not, right?" Michael grinned at her.

"That's what the guys are for," she said.

Their duel of wits ended when Liz and Joe emerged from the cabin, toilet kits in hand and towels tossed over their shoulders. Both had traveled throughout a long day and needed buffing up, as Joe termed it.

"Have you got enough quarters?" Doris asked. The public showers required five of them for exactly five minutes of hot water. Not a second more.

"I'm okay," said Joe, "but I doubt Liz's shorts'd stay up if she had enough for her."

"Don't be a smart-ass," Liz replied, then flashed him the special smile she reserved for keeping her guys in line.

Doris said, "If we're not here when you get back, join us over on the *Vega.* Inspector Clouseau here has to reopen the Hawke investigation."

Both *kids* as Michael chose to call them, exchanged puzzled glances.

Liz whispered to Joe, "Don't answer. I know that tone of voice. Mom's trying to set us up," then to Doris in a louder voice, a simple, "Okay, Mom."

Their parents watched admiringly as their children walked west along segment I of the floating dock maze that accommodated upward of two hundred pleasure craft. *Vietvet* ranked in the bottom twenty-five percent size-wise, but number one in class, likely the reason for Frederick Hawke's invitation.

Liz and Joseph turned left toward the showers at the head of the pier and disappeared.

An hour later, *Vietvet's* crew of four climbed aboard *Vega* and mounted one of the pair of teakwood circular stairs, ladders as termed by the crew. Liz wore white shorts with a red tank top and her mom a blue pullover and white pants. The men, *uniformed* per an earlier Liz observation, chose khaki shorts and similar colored Ralph Lauren polo shirts. They walked onto an open aft deck adjoining the Captain's Mess, a beautifully appointed room where twenty or so guests moved about quite comfortably. A variety of hors d'oeuvres covered the lower of a stack of handsome mahogany bookshelves surrounding the room, retainers in place to keep the books from falling out in heavy seas. At the forward end, the man who had earlier handled *Vietvet's* lines tended a well stocked bar. A woman, who Doris reckoned to be the man's wife, moved back and forth from the galley with fresh hors d'oeuvres, and to gather up empty glasses.

"Oh my God," offered the not easily impressed Liz.

Her mother observed, "Remove that expression from your vocabulary and you wouldn't get to say much."

Joe answered, "Don't make book on that, Doris."

Doris replied, "You gotta be observant to know that after only five hours, Joseph."

The remark drew an exasperated "Mom!" from Liz.

Frederick Hawke noticed his new guests and approached for introductions.

"Ah, skipper," he said to Michael. "How do you come by so beautiful and handsome a crew?"

Michael not famous for quick answers, relied on Doris. "Luck beats skill every time, Frederick."

"And a sense of humor! Skipper, I envy you. Now over here to sample Isabel's magnificent delights. I'd sooner sail without a compass than leave her ashore. Come along, you'll see why."

Joseph, unnourished for seven hours with appetite enhanced by odors from the galley could barely restrain himself. But an officer and gentleman, he waited for Liz and Doris to get into the cheese rolls before attacking the prawns and cocktail sauce. Michael watched his son with envy. Age had not diminished his appetite but added to the adverse effects of slaking it. At fifty-five, maintaining a reasonable figure meant being hungry a lot.

"Oh look!" declared Liz. "Isn't that one of your books, Michael?" Liz had dropped the Professor Kincaid title after less than an hour. She pointed to the back of a hardbound jacket that proclaimed *Pandora's Death* in block letters above the name Harry Steele.

"Harry Steele!" Frederick exclaimed. "You're the famous author? I have every one of your books and they're all aboard." He gestured about the shelves. "There's *Broken Pendant* and *Artful Murder*. You'll autograph them for me, please?"

"Of course," said Michael. *Wonder why anyone even bothers with a pen name?*

From his station behind the bar, Miguel Vargas raised his eyes on hearing Michael's nom de plume. He studied Michael an instant then lowered his eyes to uncork a fresh bottle of Kendall Jackson Chardonnay, the only non-Washington State label permitted aboard *Vega*.

Several guests clustered about for introductions, obviously fans. Others, brows furrowed in confusion, returned to their own venues with scarcely a thought to why their host had interrupted them. *It's clear John Grisham has nothing to worry about,* Michael noted.

"Are you doing a new one?" asked Roberta Walters, longtime friend of the Hawkes.

"About halfway through *Missing Person,* a novel set right here in Washington State. Ought to be out in a month or so."

"How can I get ten autographed copies? What an easy way to resolve Christmas present dilemma. We live in Port Ludlow," Roberta continued.

"I'm in Port Angeles," Michael replied.

"It's not all that far," she said. "We can drive up and meet you. Leo loves to ride, don't you, Leo?"

Leo grimaced in response to the idea.

"Sure," Michael replied. "Here's my card. Give me a call and we'll set something up."

As a second couple approached, Liz stepped up and took Michael's arm. She batted her eyes seductively. "This is my friend, author Harry Steele, aka Michael Kincaid who moonlights as a college professor."

Her remark drew an infrequent laugh from Michael. This time he had a quick rejoinder. "And this is my agent, Liz Baker."

"I thought you were the straight man," she said through a mock injured expression.

Frederick excused himself to respond to a summons from Miguel Vargas.

The man of the waiting couple made introductions. "Ben Schulz, and my better half, Ceely." He shook Michael's hand warmly. "Didn't I just read where you were involved in solving a real case? The old Blackwood murder?"

"I was involved, but credit the Clallam County Sheriff Department for cracking it. It would be fair to say they did it in spite of me."

"Well congratulations on your books. I haven't read them all, but I enjoyed the ones I did."

Liz cast about the room and noticed several other young people. She nudged Joseph, who enjoyed the limelight of his dad's adulation. "C'mon," she whispered. "Let's see if we can stir something up."

On a roll, Ben Schulz did not let go. Assuring himself Frederick could no longer hear because he had involved himself in an apparent heated discussion with Miguel, Ben said, "You know, Michael, a look into Thomas Hawke's death might be worth your while."

"Didn't the San Juan County Sheriff Department find it accidental?"

"Not a very high-tech finding, if you ask me. Not sure how much stuff they can afford up here in the islands."

Michael knew the right people and equipment to be but a few air miles away and would be called in if needed. He had no wish to continue this conversation, so did not mention this.

"Look," said the persistent Ben. "This is the third anniversary of Thomas's death, almost to the day. Frederick assembles this crowd every year about this time. Most of these guests were here at the time of Hawke's murder."

"Accidental death," Michael corrected.

"Talk to these folks; I doubt you'll find many who agree with that. I'll make you a list of names with their boats and where they're moored."

"Do that if you like, but no promises. I'm on vacation."

"I know," said Ben Schulz. "If you feel like talking about it, Ceely and I are good for a cocktail and whatever. Look for the *Yakima Gold* on the far side of the Marina." He disappeared with Ceely onto the afterdeck.

How ironic this had even come up. Doris, of course! Over their short acquaintance, her uncanny intuition had impressed him. And less than an hour ago, she had suggested this case might be in the cards. He said to her, "See the can of worms you opened?"

"Me?" said Doris, feigning astonishment with open hand upon her chest and rolling eyes.

Frederick returned with a friend who Doris had previously noticed made rounds of the hors d'oeuvre trays like a shark on a feeding frenzy.

"Peter Bushnell," said Frederick. "Meet the lovely Doris and her fortunate friend, Michael, author of the famous Harry Steele mystery novels."

After an exchange of handshakes, Frederick explained, "Peter's family and mine go back a long way and have a common bond: the products of eastern Washington's bountiful orchards."

"The Hawkes are a bit more bountiful than the Bushnells," Peter added, "as can be seen by comparing *Vega* with my twenty-seven foot Ranger moored in the *ghetto* over there." Peter gestured toward the guest docks.

Frederick jested, "But Peter's sleek *Sunskip* gets many more miles to the gallon than our *Vega,* a cumbersome beauty but completely unable to deploy a sail."

"Sail her up here alone?" Doris asked.

"No. I got a sailing buddy. A seventy-five-year-old one-legged submarine veteran. We brought the boat up from Shilshole Marina in Seattle."

"On the rags all the way?" Michael asked, using the new term learned from his son that very afternoon.

"Only way the chief will have it. Took a day, a night, and most of another day."

"Overnight? Sounds scary," added Michael.

Peter replied, "Scares the hell out of me. But the chief says it's easier to remain undetected after dark. I guess you can take submarines away from the chief, but you can't take the chief away from submarines.

"The chief?" Doris asked.

"Yeah. A Chief Quartermaster retired with thirty years service in 1967."

"Then he was in World War II," said Michael.

"Don't get him started. He was twenty-one at Pearl Harbor on a submarine. Made nine war patrols, and if you believe the chief, sank more Japanese ships than they even had. He refers to all boats except submarines as targets."

Doris suggested, "Maybe he got a few of ours by mistake to make the numbers come out."

The source of Liz's sense of humor became clear to Michael.

"The chief lose his leg in the war?" Michael asked.

"A farming accident. He claimed after thirty years of playing sailor, it was time to get a real job."

"Why did he pick eastern Washington?" Doris asked.

"According to the chief, he was tired of the sea and wanted to live in a place far enough inland that nobody even knew what it was. So he put a pair of oars on his shoulders, started at the Washington coast and walked east. Somewhere around Yakima, a farmer stopped him and asked him to identify those things on his shoulders. He set them down, bought a lot, built a house, and left the oars on his front lawn. Claims if anyone ever asks him why he has those oars on his front lawn, he'll pick them up and start walking east again."

Michael exclaimed, "Now there's a salty dog! But I've heard the tale before, so don't credit the chief for that one."

Peter nodded. "The guy who told you probably heard it from the chief."

Doris asked, "Any problems having only one leg?"

"Only ashore. It's worth ten bucks to watch the chief use the public shower. He's got to get his stool set up, lay his soap, shampoo and towel in a place he can reach them from his stool without getting the towel wet. Then he's got to figure out how to insert five quarters, pop his prosthesis off, stow it in a dry place, then get himself seated on the stool, all before his five minutes are up."

Doris laughed at the image this conjured up in her mind.

"And consider this. He's got to do it all in the buff. The chief isn't what you'd call petite. Picture a three hundred pound amoeba caught in a high speed revolving door."

Michael burst into laughter, while Doris looked about for something to hang onto.

When recomposed, Michael asked, "How come he's not here?"

"Simple. Frederick doesn't serve Remy-Martin Cognac. So, rather than drink up this good stuff gratis, the chief heads over to the Madrona Café Bar and shells out eight bucks a pop." Michael said, "Sounds like a guy I'd like to meet."

"Come over to the ghetto anytime."

"Think I will."

"Well look, it's either the chief's tacos, or these hors d'oeuvres for dinner tonight. That's a no-brainer. I better get hopping before these damn freeloaders finish off all the good stuff."

"Glad we came?" Michael asked Doris, now totally recomposed.

Joseph walked back among an array of the classiest pleasure craft he had ever seen. Liz had dispatched him to the grocery store at the head of the dock with instructions to purchase a block of ice, that he carried in a plastic bag. *Wow!* He thought. *She should teach leadership at Annapolis!* He had never known anyone with such ability to get people to do what she wanted.

Liz sat on the fantail of *Vietvet* among several young people she had collected from aboard the *Vega*. She spotted Joe and declared, "Okay, everybody! Get ready to luge." She addressed the group she'd assembled, all in their mid-twenties lavishing Coronas with slices of lime. Enthusiasm and conversation levels had increased in proportion to the number of Coronas downed.

"Okay, Joe. Find us a table to set up over … what did you call this thing?"

"Binnacle stand." Joe stood erect and raised his hand in a crisp salute. "Aye, aye, Ma'am," he snapped.

"And bring a towel!"

"Aye, aye, Ma'am!"

Joe returned with a small collapsible table intended for a light meal set up on the dock.

"Well, spread the towel across it," she admonished. Joe again complied with her instructions. Next, she directed him to set the ice block on the towel and asked for a spoon. He went to the galley and returned with one. Liz scratched grooves in a Y-shape from one end of the block to the other then set the spoon under the block below the top of the Y to create a downhill run and went below. Liz returned with a fifth of vodka, jug of orange juice, and two shot glasses. She filled one shot glass with vodka and the other with orange juice.

"You first, Leonard."

A dark-haired young man rose. "Okay, but what?"

"Put your mouth at the bottom of the Y and drink what comes out," she ordered.

Leonard complied, and Liz concurrently emptied the contents of each shot glass into the top of the Y, orange juice on one side, vodka on the other. The liquids converged at the junction, mixed, chilled, flowed to the bottom of the Y and into the waiting mouth of Leonard.

Frederick stood on the afterdeck of *Vega* and shared Doris and Michael's admiration of the vista. The Roche Harbor headland contained remains of John McMillin's lime empire, specifically, several kilns once used to convert raw limestone into a useable form for concrete, and several buildings. The once plush McMillin residence, now housed a class restaurant and the Madrona Café. The general store had become a grocery, public showers, and the small Lime Kiln Café for patrons in need of breakfast, lunch and snacks. Nothing remained of the industry that once marred the countryside and denuded San Juan Island of its trees to fire the insatiable kilns. This process dwindled to an end in the late thirties; second growth Douglas firs and cedars now reclaimed the island. At the head of the dock, five flags flew, Roche Harbor, the Washington State flag, Canada, the United Kingdom, and the United States flag in the position of honor on the truck. A chapel, Our Lady of the Good Voyage, salvaged by the Tarte family, founders of the present day resort, stood off to the east side of the community. At 9:00 a.m., 12:00 noon and 6:00 p.m., an angelus struck the hour, followed by a medley of Irish songs that floated out over the harbor. Each Sunday morning, a Roman Catholic celebration of the Mass is held at 10:15 a.m.

"You must visit the McMillin Restaurant," Frederick suggested. "For you, Doris, everything is exquisite. But Michael! The prime rib is to die for."

Michael's eyes brightened at the prospect. "Thank you very much for your hospitality," he said, extending his hand.

"And thank you for your good company and superb mysteries. You honor *Vega* with your presence," Frederick replied, not to be outdone. "And you show me Michael's talent for writing is subordinate to the one by which he selects companions," he said to Doris.

His attentiveness made her uncomfortable, but she accepted the compliment graciously.

Frederick continued, "And don't miss the colors ceremony at sunset. The concept conceived by the late Hugh Tarte is performed each night of the season by members of the Roche Harbor Marina Staff."

Extending their appreciation again, Doris and Michael departed.

"Well, where to for dinner?" Michael asked.

"Think the Lime Kiln is still open for maybe a burger?" she replied, and then watched his face fall.

"I don't like to see a grown man cry," she said. "I saw the look in your eyes when Frederick described the prime rib."

"Shall we invite the kids?" Michael asked.

"If we can find them."

They began to walk along the dock and Ben Schulz overtook them.

"Here," he said. "The list. You ought to look it over and talk to some of these people." Ben thrust a folded paper napkin into Michael's hand.

"I'm a novelist. Not a detective."

"Just like you weren't a detective on the Blackwood case?" Ben Schulz left them and returned to the *Vega*.

Doris and Michael stopped at *Vietvet* and found the luge party to have wound down, several of the young people showing obvious effects.

Doris asked her daughter, "How you guys doing?"

"Great till Second Lieutenant Party-Poop put the vodka away," Liz complained.

Michael observed, "From the looks of things, he might have been a little late. You two want to join us for dinner?"

"No thanks, Dad. There's a bachelorette party at the Madrona Liz wants to crash."

Michael cautioned, "Easy on the sauce. Okay?"

"Yes, sir," Joseph replied in a voice that meant he would comply.

Liz teased, "Our chaperone."

Doris added, "From the looks of things, you all could use one."

"It's okay, Mrs. Baker," Leonard said with a reasonably steady voice. "We'll take it easy."

"Yeah," Liz added. "Joe is the designated driver. He'll bring everybody back in a dock cart. C'mon, Mom. We can take care of ourselves."

Doris gave her daughter a stern look then continued on to the McMillin Restaurant with Michael. Soon a hostess seated them near a window overlooking the harbor.

Michael sensed her tension over Liz's behavior. "Maybe we should've come alone the first time?"

"Nope," she replied. "If anything's to become of us, it will become of everybody, and don't forget to add my son, Ralph Jr., to the mix."

"You're right," Michael agreed.

Doris lowered her eyes to the menu. "So, let's get you that rib. And maybe I'll try the salmon." Doris had a way of letting him know when the time had come to change the topic. She simply changed it, and that was that.

Dinner finished, they wandered downstairs to find Liz and Joseph doing a lively dance number to the tune of a song neither Doris nor Michael recognized.

Liz saw them and yelled, "The campus police will be by the boat soon! So no hanky-panky you two!"

Michael grinned at her. "What a spirited young woman," he said. "Get that from her mother?"

"Don't even think about going there."

"Just thought I'd take a shot."

"Well don't think. You'll weaken the team."

Satisfied the *kids* were okay, Doris and Michael left the restaurant via the bar. They noticed an elderly gentleman seated upon a bar stool behind a snifter of cognac. White hair frizzled out from the side of his large head Red Skelton style; a prosthesis hung from the left pant leg of his shorts which really did not become him. He appeared as a huge olive impaled upon an equally large toothpick. *Peter Bushnell wasn't yanking us around. There really is a chief,* Michael mused.

A few moments before sunset, they walked to the parade grounds to watch the colors ceremony as Frederick had recommended. A party of four youngsters, clad in white slacks and green pullovers marched across a well manicured lawn to recorded music of the *Colonel Bogey March*. When the music subsided, each took a halyard. Then to the bugle call *retreat*, the honor guard lowered the Roche Harbor flag, followed by the Washington State flag accompanied by the bugle call, *colors*. As the Canadian and United Kingdom flags lowered, the music of respective national anthems was played. Michael stood at rigid attention as the honor guard lowered the United States flag to the accompaniment of the bugle call, *taps*. It brought to Michael's mind a number of good friends and great Marines he had left behind in Vietnam. Suddenly, he had to blink back a tear and immediately felt Doris's hand take his.

"Are you okay, Michael?"

He didn't answer until the last note of *taps* had sounded. "Of course," he said simply. As they walked along the dock, Doris made no move to remove her hand; this pleased him. They had not previously shared this symbol of affection.

When they reached their boat, the *Vega* line handler-barkeep greeted them. "Good evening, Señor Kincaid. I am Miguel Vargas, crew Chief of the *Vega*. I am sent to advise you Señor Hawke has made his auto available for you tomorrow if you choose to explore the island."

"Thank you, Miguel. Please tell Mr. Hawke he is indeed kind and we'd enjoy that very much."

"I will, Senor." Miguel nodded then began to walk away. He stopped and turned. "Señor Kincaid, this I know for sure. My beloved padrone, Thomas Hawke, did not die by accident. He was murdered."

Chapter 3

Doris and Michael sat in the compact, but well-appointed mess deck in *Vietvet*. A table of beautifully finished mahogany dominated the setting, but able to be hinged up and secured to open the space for other activity. Ada, Jim Epsom's wife, a gifted seamstress, had contoured appropriately colored amber and gold cushions to the benches. Two glasses straddled a half filled bottle of Grand Marnier, Doris's favorite liqueur. Failing to share this preference with Michael before the trip, she brought along a bottle.

She asked, "So, what did you think of Miguel Vargas?"

Michael replied, "He's a fine line handler and even better barkeep."

"Oh c'mon, Michael. About what he said."

"Bottom line, you want me to look into this. Right?"

"It would make for a fun weekend. And where's the harm? I always wanted to play Dr. Watson. I loved Holmes's line before each climax. 'Hurry, Watson. The game's afoot.'"

Michael used his serious voice. "Well, this game is not afoot. Matter of fact, it's not even a game."

"Like father, like son. Lieutenant Party-Poop puts away the vodka bottle; the poor man's Inspector Clouseau deprives his girlfriend of her favorite fantasy."

Michael's face brightened. "You're my girlfriend?"

"Pure logic. I'm a girl, and you're my friend."

"Figures," Michael replied. "So, you want to play the game? How do you suggest we proceed?"

"Start by looking at the people on Ben Schulz's list."

"And what will we get from that, apart from a bunch of wild theories?"

Michael hoped to subdue her with pure wisdom and experience.

"See a lot of nice boats and maybe get invited to a lunch or two."

Doris sipped her GM, savoring its sweetness and body.

"Can't fault that. Maybe I should write in a lady companion to help Harry work his cases."

"You mean instead of those round heeled bimbos you fix him up with?"

Michael asked, "How can a guy be comfortable around a woman who knows that much about him? I'll go along if we can start with Peter Bushnell. I sure want to meet the chief."

"Out of the mouths of babes. You read my mind, Michael."

"I wouldn't bank on lunch from him."

"From what Peter told us, don't think we want any. Let's do him early. If coffee's in the cards, we can always sip and run."

Michael said, "You're on. The game's afoot, but only for the time being. Now, if we only had a few suspects and any evidence at all to show Thomas Hawke met with foul play."

"Sergeant Major Party-Poop?"

"You don't let up, do you, Doris?"

Michael changed the subject and got into a topic most awkward for him. "The purpose of this trip is to get the four of us to know each other, right?"

"Yes," she replied tentatively.

"That includes you and me?"

"As long as I'm not cast as one of Steele's round heels."

"You don't make anything easy, do you?"

She caught the edge in his voice. "Sorry, Michael. It's just you make so many openings; you're a comedienne's dream come true."

She's fun to be around, no doubt about that, Michael thought. Then said, "This romance thing."

Though Doris warmed to him at this juncture, the remark struck her as funny. She struggled, but successfully masked her reaction.

"Yes?" She replied in an even voice, aware humor was her favorite stress reliever.

Michael began, "It's been a long time for me."

Even longer for me, she thought. "Go on."

"All the tricks in my bag are dated; you'd see right through them. It's been twenty-five years since I've tried to impress a woman and didn't do a decent job even then."

"Then why not leave things just the way they are?"

"I guess I want a relationship. Not that we don't have one." Michael knew he did a poor job of speaking his mind, and did not wish to appear an ass to Doris. He cleared his head and spoke like he would to a class. "Candidly, most of the sand is at the bottom of my hourglass. This is a selfish but truthful assessment. I don't want to spend the rest of what's left alone. I've done far too much of that already."

Doris shared this feeling, a major difference being she had her children to focus on and expended much energy there. Michael owned little more than his four walls and only dreams of his son. Michael married a woman after a one-night stand. Pregnancy resulted. During his Vietnam tour, the woman divorced him and arranged for adoption at birth without Michael's permission. Many years passed before Michael found the boy, happy in a foster home, and he had no wish to disrupt that.

"That's reasonable, Michael." She reached across the table and signaled him to put his hand in hers. "I agree. We're too far along in life for the traditional courtship."

For an instant, a vision of whooping cranes in a mating dance ritual ran through her mind and she bit her lip. But she could not contain the smile this put on her face. Fortunately, Michael construed it as a special one for him.

She continued with, "I always liked this line from a letter Amelia Earhart wrote to her husband, George Putnam, a short time before they were married. 'My fear is that I will not do what others want me to do or expect from me.' I construe this to mean he should not expect her to follow or lead, but they should walk together side by side. Maybe that's what we need to do. A little side by side first and see how we like the trip."

He nodded his assent, and then a puzzled look spread over his face. "But how am I doing?"

"One thing sure hasn't changed. Guys still need to be stroked. You do just fine, Michael. You've showed me a lot, and I like what I see."

He gave her hand a squeeze. "A two-way street if there ever was one."

Heavy stomping on the main deck shattered their mood.

In her best attempt at a deep masculine voice Liz demanded, "Okay, what's happening down there?"

"You don't want to know," Michael responded. "Give us a few seconds to get some clothes on."

Doris exclaimed, "Michael!"

Liz and Joseph came below and two more Grand Marniers were poured. After shared accounts of their respective evenings, the ladies retired to the plush main cabin while the men converted the dining area into a bunkroom.

Michael announced, "Coffee here then to the Lime Kiln Café for breakfast."

Mother's and daughter's voices in chorus floated through the closed cabin door, "No arguments."

Joseph said, "The mention of food reels Liz right in."

Silence a few seconds then Liz called from the main cabin, "You know I'll get even for that."

He answered, "What else is new?"

Michael used his best drill sergeant voice. "Lights out and silence about the decks!"

Fresh air from the sail over the Strait combined with the rest of their hectic day's activities sent everyone into a sound sleep.

A short line at Lime Kiln Café found the four quickly seated behind their favorite breakfasts: perfect eggs up, crisp bacon, warm whole-wheat toast and steaming coffee for Michael, scrambled eggs and sausage for the women, and a plate obscured by a stack of pancakes with a side dish of sausages sat before Joseph.

"And this is the man who says food reels me in. Saving some of that for lunch, Joe? They got doggie bags that big?"

Joseph took Liz easily in stride by now. Her remark did not diminish the ferocity of his attack on breakfast.

Doris asked, "How can you put that much away without it showing?"

Michael answered, "Joseph's metabolism has a metabolism of its own," then said, "Mr. Hawke has offered the use of a car today, if anybody wants to take him up on it."

Doris said, "There's more to San Juan Island than what you can see from the Strait."

"Count me in," said Joseph, barely able to speak through his mouthful.

"Me too," said Liz.

Joseph took a breath. "My roommate at Annapolis said he's from Anacortes. There are some people thinking about setting up a winery on the island. Maybe we can check it out."

Michael replied, "Good luck to them. This is not the best climate for growing grapes."

"I know. Byron, my roomy, says they'll ship grapes in from eastern Washington, just like the other companies out here. But there's a German grape, Siegerrebe, that does well in this climate."

Liz asked, "How does Lieutenant PP know so much about wine?"

Joseph took another bite of pancake. "Just repeating what I heard."

Doris said, "Well, sounds like it's shaping up to be a good day."

Michael interjected. "But first, Nick and Nora Charles have some business to take care of."

The *kids* reacted to Michael's remark with a pair of equally confused looks.

He went on, "You know … The Thin Man."

Doris said, "Michael, you can't expect them to know who they are. It was before my time and I learned about them only after I became a public television old movies junkie." Directing her remarks to Liz and Joseph, Doris went on, "They were a husband and wife detective team in a popular mystery series of the thirties and forties."

"Wow, Dad ... husband and wife team. This mean you're gonna make an honest woman of Doris?"

Michael protested, "Okay, okay."

Liz sustained her penchant for getting in the last word. "Lieutenant PP continues to surprise us. First, wine expert ... now, comedian. Is there no end to this man's talents?"

Though none of the four had expressed the thought, each continued to enjoy their time at Roche.

Doris and Michael began sleuthing shortly after breakfast. First visit: *Sunskip*, Peter Bushnell's sailboat. They found it jammed into a tight, unmarked space on the guest dock. An add-on, the section pontoon tops hovered closer to the water's edge than the other segments. This worked for the chief whose prosthesis handled straight and level sailing pretty well, but didn't like negotiating a down step from dock to boat without a handrail. One foot on the dock and the other on the relatively small boat, made *Sunskip* move away from the dock before the other foot could be raised. The closer the dock level to the gunwale, the better.

Beneath a blue tarp spread over *Sunskip's* boom, shirtless and wearing a pair of shorts, the chief presented an unsightly apparition.

"Good morning, Chief. I'm Michael Kincaid. Your sailing buddy, Peter Bushnell, said you'd be moored here."

The chief asked, "Bushnell? Went up to chapel to shed a tear for Admiral Nimitz."

Michael recognized the Navy idiom for going to the can for a whiz.

"And this is Mrs. Baker. May we come aboard and visit?"

"Oops," said the chief. "Didn't see you, Ma'am. Yes, come aboard." He looked at his Bud Light. "Can I get you a brew?"

"No thanks," Michael replied for them both. "Sun's not over the yardarm yet."

"Must be someplace in the world," the chief replied, raising his nearly empty can in emphasis. Anything I can do for you?"

"Matter of fact, there is. I'm a part-time private detective and Mrs. Baker—"

"Doris," she corrected.

"Doris is my assistant."

She raised her eyes at the term assistant but didn't push it.

"We've been asked to look into the death of Thomas Hawke. I understand some believe it might not have been an accident."

The chief squinted first at Michael then at Doris. "Who thinks that?"

"Miguel Vargas, for one. He said there were others. Does that include you?"

"You oughtn't listen to Miguel. His elevator doesn't go all the way to the top floor. But to answer your question, I'd have no way of knowin'."

Michael asked, "Were you here the night he died?"

"Yep. Peter and me both. Moored right here, we were."

"What do you remember about it?"

"Nothing. Only a big commotion over on J dock. Every cop in San Juan County was here. A wonder the damn thing didn't sink from the sheer weight of them. Sure you won't have a brew?"

The chief pulled a fresh one for himself from the cooler at the rear of the cockpit. Though not spacious, *Sunskip* afforded comfortable seating for three. The chief and Peter made good use of the limited room and despite a rough exterior, the chief liked for things to be tidy. It had become deeply rooted during his days in submarines that had room aboard for everything but a mistake.

Doris placed a hand on the chief's arm, looked at him and asked, "How do you feel about it personally, Chief?"

"If he was murdered, somebody had to do it for a reason. Guess his son had good cause, but it was pretty much confirmed he was on the mainland driving to Seattle when Thomas died."

"How was that?" Michael asked.

"Two witnesses in his car at the time fixed for Thomas's death. Hitchhikers he picked up on the ferry to Anacortes."

Doris arched her eyebrows toward Michael and wondered. *How hard would it be to buy that kind of testimony? Frederick certainly had the bucks.*

The chief quickly torpedoed her theory. "Thomas ran him off from here with barely lunch money. Flat broke, he was."

Michael considered the witnesses' stories were checked nine ways from Sunday before the San Juan County Sheriff Department let Frederick off the hook. They had to be airtight.

Doris enjoyed the game immensely and wondered. *What would Nora Charles ask?* "What is your and Peter's connection to the Hawkes?"

"Peter mainly. Both in the fruit business. Thomas a bit quicker than Peter. You can see what a difference that made. You were aboard *Vega* last night, I hear. Thomas's quickness accounts for the difference between his boat and this."

Jealousy can be a powerful motive. Doris asked "How does Peter feel about that?" She sensed the chief enjoyed the attention she paid him. *Use my girly wiles on him. That's what Nora would do.* She wondered if Michael emulated Harry Steele with equal vigor. Nora probably would not have gotten along with the blunt detective in Michael's books. She preferred Nick the sophisticate.

The chief said, "If Peter had the Hawke fortune, he'd still sail in *Sunskip*. He loves this boat."

She thought, *Another theory bites the dust.*

Michael asked, "How did you and Peter hook up, Chief?"

"You can retire on CPO pay, but don't try to live on it. I needed a job and Peter had plenty of work."

"How about the sailing?"

"Here comes Peter. Let him tell you," the chief replied.

The thump of Peter's white boat shoes rocked the floating dock as he approached. "Good morning, Doris and—"

"Michael," she helped, knowing he would otherwise be left hanging with his greeting.

"Michael ... yes. Did you have a nice dinner?"

"Superb," Doris admitted.

"So, what good breeze brings you to *Sunskip*?"

Michael related the tale of their encounter with Miguel the previous evening and their decision to play detective for the weekend. "After all you told us last night, what better person to start with than the chief and, of course, you ... what was your name?"

Peter replied, "Touché."

Michael said, "It's all right, Peter. If it were me, I'd also be too preoccupied with Doris to remember her friend's name too."

The remark earned him a smile from Doris. She thought, *Maybe Harry Steele does have a bit of Nick Charles in him.*

Michael went on. "The chief said I should ask you about how the two of you started to sail together."

"It's a long story. I learned to sail on Moses Lake in central Washington when I was a boy. Then when the Hawkes hit it big, they discovered Roche Harbor and established the custom of exposing the riffraff to paradise one weekend a year. It made me want to do it on my own. I knew the sailing part, but navigation was another story. That's where the chief came in. *Sunskip* was moored at Shilshole Marina in Seattle. I bought her after he assured me that if he could find a speck in the Pacific Ocean that was Hawaii with nothing more than a sextant and clock, getting us up to Roche was a piece of cake. True to his word, he's found it every time."

The chief gave his buddy a look slightly short of a scowl then said half seriously, "Once he gets all the fancy electronic stuff, I expect he'll dump me."

Peter replied, "If it's like the rest of the gear we have aboard it'll crap out every now and again. When it happens, especially at night, I'll need the chief to figure out where we are. Plus, he's pretty damn good at keeping us from running into things."

Michael knew of the work in need of doing topside while making up, hoisting, and dousing sail. Though the chief had good mobility, with any kind of a sea running, it would be too dangerous for him to go forward onto the main deck. The chief would be of little help in performing these essential tasks. Michael sensed a deep friendship between the two accounted for why they sailed together.

Michael put the train back on the tracks. "Did you know Thomas very well, Peter?"

"I was two grades behind him all the way through school. Our families migrated to the tri-cities area at about the same time a century ago."

Doris considered Peter's allusion to riffraff wondering if this could be a lead. "You give me the impression Hawke lorded his success over the rest of you."

"You could say that. Kinda natural, though. If it were the other way round, I'd likely do the same thing."

Aha, Doris thought. *A little difference between the chief's and Peter's answers. Another lead? Nora would be proud.*

Liz and Joseph lingered over coffees at the Lime Kiln after their parents left. "So, tell me about the Marines, Joe. Sounds exciting."

"So far, so good. Just finished nine weeks of basic infantry school."

"So you're good to go now?"

"I learned to find myself a good platoon sergeant and do what he tells me till I get my bearings," Joe replied. "I'm interested in aviation, but the Marines are primarily ground pounders."

"Ground pounders?"

"Yeah. Infantry troops. Operate on land. I figure the Airedales support ground troops, so it might not be a bad idea to learn what they need before going off and learning how to provide it."

"Sounds good. But the Marines have a way of being the first involved. Seemed I heard as much about them in Desert Storm as I did the Army. How do you feel about that?"

"I'm young and dumb enough to still think that sounds exciting. But when I listened to the combat vets that taught at Annapolis … well, I'm not all that sure. I guess where I'm at right now, is I'd certainly go if called, but have learned enough to know I'm really not ready to lead troops in combat. And I'd hate to be responsible for losing people because I didn't know what I was doing."

Joseph had become so serious it even made the flippant Liz uncomfortable. She liked being with Joe, but maybe there's too much risk in a friendship with someone who might go off and get himself killed. The angelus in the cupola atop Our Lady of the Good Voyage Chapel struck 9:00 a.m., followed by a rendition of Danny Boy on the bells. Liz had sung this song as part of a chorus in high school and recalled it to be a song of grief by an Irish father who sent his son off to war.

She changed the subject. "Tell me about your roommate from Anacortes. How did he find out about wine here on the Island?"

"Byron's an avid cyclist. He liked San Juan Island because it doesn't have very many hills. He and his buddies would take their bikes on the ferry and come over here for weekends. They brought sleeping bags and slept over in a barn owned by a couple who talked about setting up a winery."

"Any idea where that might be?"

Joseph replied, "No, but we could ask around."

Liz suggested, "Maybe we should check into some bikes and give the lovebirds some time alone. They haven't had a lot of that."

He liked the idea. Not for Liz's reasoning, but the idea of an afternoon alone with her had great appeal. "I think I can get a pass from the sergeant major, but how about the Dean's hatchet?"

"I can't wait to hear you call her that, Joe."

"Uh-oh, watch your wallets," he said in a voice loud enough for Doris and Michael to hear as they approached the table.

Michael said, "Saddle up the troops, Lieutenant. We're moving out."

"The Lieutenant countermands that order, Sergeant Major. Ms. Baker and the Lieutenant will turn the island's south flank mounted on bicycles while the Sergeant Major and the Dean's hatchet reconnoiter Friday Harbor by motorized vehicle."

Doris exclaimed, "Dean's hatchet!"

Liz said to Joseph, "I told you."

Chapter 4

Doris and Michael sat in the outdoor section of a restaurant overlooking the ferry dock at Friday Harbor. Across San Juan Channel, Lopez Island sat about a mile distant beyond fifty or so pleasure craft availing themselves of a spectacular afternoon. Not a cloud marred the deep azure sky and a mild breeze blew gently across the channel to the delight of many sailboaters.

Doris and Michael watched auto and foot-traffic finish boarding the ferry then listened to the ferry's deep voice as she moved out of her slip en route to Anacortes. Her white superstructure, green hull, squat and graceless ... its full size realized only while passing close to pleasure boats as it moved its way among them.

Boats under sail have the right of way over power boats, but Michael had learned from Jim Epsom that tonnage beats Rules of the Road every time. The sailboats appeared to agree, as they tacked to give the ferry her needed sea room. Jim also reckoned that, *these guys are out here to make a living. We're only here to play, so let's keep out of their way.* This made a great deal of sense to Michael.

Liz and Joseph were off biking and would be famished by the time they returned to Roche.

Though only early afternoon, Doris said, "We should get something light, Michael, if we expect to match the kids at dinner."

She suggested they share a crab cake, to be washed down by a tall, cool Alaskan Amber Ale, a popular product of a microbrewery in that state. Michael agreed, though without obvious zeal. When lunch arrived, his expression showed disappointment over its meager size.

She took pity on Michael, a big man who had breakfasted too lightly in her view. This made him far too hungry at lunch, which in turn gave him a tendency to overeat. Doris had not reached the point where she would be comfortable telling him that.

"You can have my roll," she offered.

He smiled his appreciation. "No, thanks. Actually, I can do with a bit more living off the hump. The damn dry cleaner keeps shrinking the waistband on my trousers."

She agreed, but did not express this view. "Where do you get all these great one liners?"

"From an old gunnery sergeant I knew back in the Corps days. He could come up with great reasons for the troops to stop feeling sorry for themselves. I refer to him as the old gunny."

"Do you know what became of him?"

"Retired by now. But hundreds of his clones are sprinkled throughout the Corps. Chaplains are good, but the old gunny … well, he was just something else."

"So where do we stand on the case?" Doris asked.

"All questions and no answers, normal for this stage of the investigation."

"I'm suspicious of Frederick. He had so much to gain from his father's death," Doris reasoned, but did not admit that Frederick annoyed her.

"The way it's supposed to work is first try to vindicate a suspect. It makes the investigation more objective and saves a lot of work in the bargain. I'd let him off the hook on the strength of the Sheriff Department findings."

Doris watched Michael look at the final bite of crab cake and insisted he have it. "I see," she said. "It can be easier to prove a suspect didn't do it and save a lot of investigation time."

"Exactly," Michael agreed. "But don't forget, ours is a double-edged sword. Was there even a murder? Prove there was before we waste time figuring out who committed it."

"So far, we've completed two interviews. What do we know from them?"

Michael thought a moment. "We haven't proved it wasn't an accident but know both Peter and the chief had motive and access to Thomas."

"Motive? I thought so too, Michael. Peter clearly resented him, and the chief's loyalty to Peter is extensive enough for him to be a suspect."

"Right, and Frederick isn't completely off the hook."

"No?" *Was Michael reversing himself?*

"He was not at the scene but could have hired someone to do the job for him. The Hawkes run a sizeable operation. It would be fairly easy to cook the books enough to hide a big payoff."

Doris said, "Makes sense to me. But the important thing … are you enjoying this? Vacations are supposed to be fun, Michael."

"I am," he replied. "And I like the new tool you add to our bag of tricks: woman's intuition."

Doris rewarded him with a smile. "So what's next?"

"We go back to Roche for more interviews. Maybe Ben Schulz and his wife … what was her name?"

"Ceely," Doris replied.

"He claims to have reason to believe it was murder. Maybe we should hear it. Another thing Harry Steele always does."

"What's that?"

"Be suspicious of the guy who tries to take himself out of suspicion by being the one who calls for the investigation. The *he doth protest too much, methinks* syndrome."

Joseph looked at Liz who pedaled ahead of him. *What a set of buns,* he thought. He set his mind at ease by reckoning himself too young to be a dirty old man, but generated appreciation for that point of view.

Liz called back to him, "Where is it, Joe?"

"Getting tired?"

"Yeah, sure." The athletic Liz had not even worked up a sweat. Curiosity, not fatigue, fueled her impatience. "You got me sold on the idea of seeing this place."

He checked his odometer. "Sign should be popping up anytime."

Before mounting up, Joseph had told her about the Pig War. How in 1859, Great Britain and the United States nearly came to serious blows because a U.S. Citizen shot a pig belonging to an English settler on San Juan Island. The U.S. and the British Dominion of Canada had settled the boundary between them at the 49th parallel. However, the boundary stopped at the southern tip of Vancouver Island, site of present day Victoria, well below the 49th.

This left the status of the San Juan Islands unresolved; hence English and American settlers defined boundaries as it best suited each. The British held the boundary ran through Rosario Strait, east of the San Juans, and the Americans claimed it to be Haro Strait to the west. The pig shooting precipitated a standoff that lasted twelve years, with U.S. and British troops concurrently occupying San Juan Island. Over this period, America had its hands full with the Civil War.

Liz exclaimed, "Right here!"

They turned down the road by a sign that proclaimed they reached the site of the British encampment. At the park entrance, Liz pedaled past a sign that read: No Bicycles Beyond This Point. Then on to a restored barracks that served as park headquarters and movie theater.

A middle-aged woman in a Park Ranger uniform said, "I'm sorry. You'll have to take your bikes back to the entrance and leave them there."

Joseph replied, "I saw the sign, but Liz, here, was too far ahead; I was trying to catch up to tell her."

Joseph felt a sharp pain in his back lower rib cage from Liz's balled fist, out of the Ranger's view.

"Ouch!"

"Goody two shoes," Liz said in a low voice.

A combination of things—likely because the Ranger had a son about Joseph's age and enjoyed the prospects of passing some time with this likeable couple—caused her to rescind. "Okay, leave the bikes here, but when you go, walk them out please."

"Yes, Ma'am," earned Joseph another hidden shot in the ribs.

Joseph noticed a rendering of General Winfield Scott, Commander of the Union Armies on the eve of the U.S. Civil War. The Pig War big enough to include Scott, surprised him.

The Ranger explained, "A number of famous people were involved. Most folks don't know George E. Pickett, of Pickett's Charge fame at the Battle of Gettysburg, was the first commander of American troops here."

Joseph asked, "Pickett? He was out here only two years before the Civil War?"

"He was," the Ranger replied.

Liz had a fascination and knowledge of history, particularly the nineteenth century and of the bleak state of communications between east and west coasts at that time. Not a single telegraph line paralleled the overland routes which improved little since the Lewis and Clark expedition.

She asked, "How did he get back to join the Confederacy?"

Joseph related, "Pickett resigned his commission and took a ship to what is now the Isthmus of Panama. There, he took a train to the east coast and another ship to Virginia where he accepted a commission in the Confederate Army."

Liz suggested, "A determined man."

"And a lot more," Joseph replied. "His life was fraught with irony. He was appointed to West Point by Abraham Lincoln, of all people. He graduated last in his class. I wonder if they sent him out here just to keep him out of the way. He married a Haida Indian woman in Bellingham, who died shortly after the birth of a son, James Tilton Pickett in 1857. Southern U.S. social structures of the time made no accommodation for what they termed a half-breed. As a consequence, James lived out his days in the Pacific Northwest and had no further contact with his father."

"Interesting," replied the woman. She made a few notes. "That's worth checking into. But General Pickett distinguished himself in the Mexican War."

"That actually tracks with several other famous officers," Joseph added. "Lee, Grant, and Custer to name just a few. Great in combat but disasters in peacetime."

Liz asked, "Then what happened to Pickett at Gettysburg? That was certainly war."

"He obeyed a bad order," Joseph replied. "He led fifteen thousand troops across an open field and lost most of them. It was the high water mark for the South in the Civil War, but not much of an achievement considering the result. Clearly, it was the handwriting on the wall for the South after that."

Fascinated with Joseph's knowledge on the subject, the Ranger asked, "What became of Pickett after that?"

"The following September, he married LaSalle Corbell in Petersburg, Virginia. She was only fifteen and he thirty-eight. A beautiful young woman by her surviving photos. She spent the rest of her life touting her husband. He needed it. Bad blood grew between him and Lee because of the Gettysburg order. A week before the war's end, Lee fired him for incompetence."

"Then what happened to him?" Liz asked.

"He became an insurance salesman and died when LaSalle was only thirty."

"Well," said Liz, "everything you ever wanted to know about George E. Pickett but were afraid to ask."

She marveled at the sensitivity shown by Joseph, but said nothing. He'd shown compassion in his account of General Pickett's trials and tribulations and the importance of describing his young wife as beautiful. Apparently nothing much evaded Joseph's curiosity; Liz liked that in a man, but considered this far too early to share such thoughts.

They toured the remaining facilities in the well-maintained park: the blockhouse, storehouse and formal gardens.

Liz commented, "I can see why duty was pretty nice here."

Joseph replied, "At least for the British. The American camp left a lot to be desired and the troops were not too happy."

Liz teased, "Is there anything you don't know?"

"Coupla things."

He smiled and left her to draw her own conclusions. He thought of the impending departure only a few days off. *Then what?*

They walked their bikes to the park entrance like a pair of Liz's *goody two shoes.*

After mounting up, Liz said, "You ride in front this time. It's my turn to watch your cute little butt."

Ben and Ceely Schulz fell over themselves to accommodate Doris and Michael's surprise visit aboard their fifty-eight-foot yacht, *Yakima Gold.*

Appearing in his late fifties and having gained some obvious weight since he bought his shorts, Ben, said, "Nice of you to come by."

Curly brown hair surrounded a circular bald spot on the back of his head but showed no gray.

A slender and pretty woman, Ceely needed cosmetic help to keep her hair dark. The four seated themselves about the *Gold's* well-appointed fantail.

Ceely opened with, "Where are your kids?"

Doris gave an account of Liz and Joseph's plans for the day.

Ben could not wait to broach the question foremost on his mind. "Have you given any thought to my list?"

A surprised Ceely asked, "Your what?"

Ben explained.

Then Michael fielded the question. "As a matter of fact, yes. Doris and I decided it might be good to work Hercule Poirot's little gray cells."

"Poirot?" asked Ben.

Doris said, "You've got to forgive Michael. He's an English literature professor who likes to show off. Poirot is an Agatha Christie character ... the detective in *Murder on the Orient Express.*"

Still confused, Ben replied, "Oh."

Ceely knew this. She'd watched many *Poirot* chapters of the series on public television while Ben watched some sporting event or other. She did not embarrass her husband, who tended to be defensive.

Michael began, "What can you tell me about the night of Thomas Hawke's death? The San Juan County Sheriff office ruled the death accidental and I find their reasons compelling."

Ben answered, "I can tell you this. Very few of the people Thomas invited to his fancy parties liked him very much."

Ceely took a breath as though she meant to say something but remained silent.

Michael asked, "Do you think they disliked him enough to murder him?"

Ben replied, "Hard to say. What's enough in one man's mind might not be in another's. That's for you to figure out."

Michael thought cynically, *Thanks a lot.* "Can you tell me more?"

Ben replied, "Sure. Do you know about the baseball bat?"

"Baseball bat?"

"Yeah. Thomas kept one behind the ice chest he had on the afterdeck. It was used to kill fish before they put them in the cooler."

"What about it?"

"It was missing the morning after Thomas's death. But they found it washed ashore two days later. None of the *Vega* crew, including Miguel Vargas knew how it had gotten into the water. Miguel was the only person besides Thomas who knew it was there. The sheriff ruled it out as the murder weapon."

Michael replied, "What about fingerprints? They'd stay on a coupla days, even in saltwater."

"Only Thomas's and Miguel's. Miguel's were explainable because he was the one who killed the fish. But somebody else could have used gloves."

Michael nodded to concede the point. "Do you think Miguel could have done it?"

"Never in a million years. Miguel's and his wife's loyalty to Thomas was the stuff of legends."

"I understand there was evidence on the deadhead that showed the fatal blow was caused when his head struck it."

"Deadhead?" Doris asked.

"A half floating log. Not much of it is seen above the waterline," Michael explained.

"Could have been put there after the fact. The killer could simply clean off the bat then bring the wound on the back of Thomas's head onto the log enough to leave residue."

Ceely declared, "Ben!"

She had no stomach for his narrative and excused herself.

Doris's mental picture conjured by Ben's description unnerved her. *Nora Charles wouldn't bat an eye,* she thought and remained composed. "Wouldn't that have been hard to pull off?"

"Easy. Dump Thomas over the side. He was already dead, so his lungs would be full of air and he'd float. Assume the killer had a skiff. He'd simply find a deadhead, Lord knows there's always plenty in the harbor, and tow it to the *Vega*. He'd have to do this with oars so nobody would hear him, but it could be done. Then whack the back of Thomas's head against it to leave evidence, and then take off. Several witnesses heard an outboard motor about that time. But the Sheriff said it was likely someone going off to check their crab pots."

Michael thought, *Or somebody else's at that hour.* "Did you share this scenario with the Sheriff?"

"Of course, but all he wanted to do was tidy up and get the thing over with. So what do you think, Mike?"

Doris and Michael exchanged glances between each other and then toward Ben who appeared troubled, likely from his quickly gathered perception of Doris's superb intuition.

Michael asked Doris, "What do you think?"

She framed her response in a new question to Ben. "Have you ever discussed this with Miguel?"

Ben replied, "No."

"Then to anyone who might have?"

"No, again. A lot of us share the opinion the Sheriff might have tied this off too quickly, but keep whatever theories we have to ourselves."

Doris nodded first to Ben, then to Michael. "Then Miguel must have reasons of his own for believing Thomas's death was not accidental. Maybe we ought to hear them."

Michael resisted the urge to declare, *Hurry Watson, the game's afoot.* He actually reckoned the circumference differences satisfied the sheriff that the deadhead and not the bat caused Thomas Hawke's fatal injury. Michael did not share this. He had no wish to stifle conjecture, an essential ingredient to thorough detective work.

Next stop for Joseph and Liz, Lime Kiln Point State Park. At the turn of the century, enough ships piled up here that the Life Guard Service—later the U.S. Coast Guard—decided to erect a lighthouse at Lime Kiln Point. A dual purpose Washington State Park had been set up; a listening post for whales in the area, and to exhibit the lighthouse, a functioning historical landmark.

The mid-sixties woman operating the listening post could barely contain her excitement over an opportunity to explain the whale listening installation.

Dressed in a State Park Uniform, she launched immediately into an explanation of a series of hydrophones planted in an underwater array some distance off shore—amplifiers and speakers. Nothing but background noise could be heard on the speaker. She explained the L-pod of Orca whales had been sighted thirty miles southeast and were headed in this direction. In Liz's view, the woman described this impending event as the single most important one of her life.

Liz asked, "Are you able to tell anything from the sounds they make? Like discovering food, which direction to move in?"

"Actually, no. We've uncovered no patterns, but as the equipment gets better, we'll be able to process ever-greater volumes of data, and something is sure to emerge. Everything animals do is for a reason."

The woman had an obvious great love for what she termed magnificent creatures.

Fortunately for Joseph, the woman turned around to adjust the speaker volume level and did not hear his next remark, well-intentioned, if not carefully thought out.

With the islands' original Native American inhabitants in mind, he asked, "Are they good to eat?"

The remark earned him another shot in the rib cage.

Liz exclaimed, "Idiot!"

Joseph wondered if a continued relationship might result in long-term chronic back pain but immediately recognized the impropriety of his comment in addition to its unplanned humor. He needed to turn his back to the woman so she could not see his stifled laughter, which he covered with a feigned coughing spasm.

They admired an impressive spread of recent photos of the L-pod.

A younger woman approached to relieve the Ranger for a lunch break. Liz watched the new arrival's expression brighten when she spotted Joseph.

"Hi. I'm Laurie," she said, extending her hand.

"I'm Joe, and this is Liz."

Handshakes were exchanged all around.

Laurie asked in a saccharine voice that annoyed Liz, "Are you finding out all you need?"

Liz replied, "This kind lady told us just about everything."

Laurie nodded. "Okay. Well, the lighthouse is not open to visitors, but seeing no one else is here, if you like, I'll take you up."

Before Liz was able to say, *No thanks, we gotta get back.* Joseph exclaimed, "That'd be great!"

Liz stood in front of him, or he would have gotten another shot in the ribs.

Laurie's glance at Liz's left hand to determine whether it bore a ring bordered on flagrant. "C'mon up," she invited.

Liz thought, *Said the spider to the fly.*

Laurie climbed the narrow circular staircase ahead of Joseph, no doubt to give him a good view of her nicely turned rear end.

Joseph explained, "We came by here on the way to Roche," then asked, "flashing white every ten seconds?"

"That's right," said Laurie as they reached the light chamber.

Joseph checked his watch to confirm the rotating lens interval while Laurie recited the history of the light. "It was originally powered by a kerosene lamp." Then pointing to a pair of buildings below, she said, "The fuel was stored in separate places, so in the event one was destroyed only half the fuel would be lost with no interruption to the service."

Joseph asked, "So, what do you do when you're not State Parking?"

"I begin my senior year at Washington State in the fall. I'm majoring in environment with a minor in wildlife."

Liz grit her teeth while Joseph oohed and aahed over each Laurie remark.

Returning to the light, he asked. "At what distance can the light be seen?"

"Seventeen miles."

"Then it's gotta be fifty some feet above the water."

"Right. Fifty-five feet. How did you know that, Joseph?"

"Height above the water equates to the distance it can be seen. There are tables for that, but a rule of thumb benchmark is eight miles for fifty feet. In figuring the distance, they normally credit a height of eye aboard ship to be approximately equal to the lighthouse. Eight and a half miles for the ship, eight and a half for the light makes seventeen."

"Wow, where did you learn that?" Laurie's words were exaggerated in proportion to everything else about her, at least in Liz's mind.

"At the Naval Academy," Joseph replied, doing a rotten job at trying to be nonchalant.

Cripes, here we go, thought Liz.

"So ... are you a Naval Officer?"

"No, Marine Corps."

Laurie exclaimed, "Wow! You guys staying at Roche? The state keeps a few rooms for us there at the resort dormitory. Maybe we can get together?"

"Sure," Joseph replied.

Liz said, "We better get moving, or we're in big trouble back at the boat."

Joseph took off down the steps.

Liz grabbed Laurie by the arm so she'd stay behind. "Laurie, you're a sweetheart! Thank you for being so kind to my patient."

"Patient?"

"Joseph suffers from seizures. I'm a nurse. Got the stuff right here in my fanny pack in case he has one."

"But the Naval Academy?"

"He's on his manic side today. Told the last people we talked to, he was Confederate General George Pickett."

"Oh my God!"

"Think that's bad?" Liz went on, "On his depressive days he believes he's Louis XVI being led to the guillotine. But he seems to like you, Laurie. Maybe you can spell me tonight so I can go have dinner with this guy I met at Roche?"

When they rejoined Joe, he asked, "Well how do we get in touch, Laurie?"

"Oh, Liz told me where you are. If I can get some time off, I'll find you."

Liz played it to the end. "Okay, General Pickett, mount up. We gotta charge those Yankees on the hill over there."

She could count on Joseph to do some dumb thing to corroborate her story.

He thrust his fist forward in a magnanimous gesture and shouted, "Follow me, men!"

Then he pedaled vigorously up the hill.

Liz turned to Laurie, shoulders shrugged, arms extended downward, and palms open. "See?"

Chapter 5

Isabel Vargas appeared to Doris as a forlorn doe. Shoulders rounded, her big brown eyes contemplated Doris and Michael from a gentle but frightened face. Doris reckoned life had not been good to Isabel before her husband Miguel came into it.

Miguel comforted his wife and said to her in Spanish, "All is well, mi espousa. These are good people. You do not have to fear them. They would like to find the person who murdered our padrone, Thomas Hawke. We must help."

The four sat in *Vega's* crew mess compartment. Michael came aboard to return the auto keys and found Frederick ashore. He used this occasion to test Miguel on his belief that Thomas Hawke met with foul play.

Doris pulled another rabbit from her bottomless hat. She spoke excellent Spanish. She added her soothing voice to Miguel's and opened by complimenting Isabel on the superb food she served the previous evening aboard *Vega*.

She went on to say, "I know it was a bad time for you, but your husband said you heard certain things on the night of Señor Hawke's death."

Isabel looked toward Miguel through an expression that approached pain.

"It is well, Isabel. You must tell them."

Isabel described the earlier sounds she heard coming from the heated discussion between Frederick and his father. "But later, there was something else."

"Tell them, Isabel. It is good for you to do that."

Doris asked, "Was it something you saw as well as heard?"

"I heard only."

Michael said, "Ask her if she recalls what time?"

Doris translated the question.

"It was 2:00 a.m.," Isabel said. "I believe all women who are mothers sleep lightly." Though their grown son Renaldo attended Med School at UW, she continued to regard him as niño. "The need to protect our children never leaves us. Even while sleeping we always guard against danger."

"So tell us," said Doris.

"Early in the evening, I heard the bad words pass between Frederick and his father. But what I heard later was not the voice of Frederick."

Miguel demanded, "How can you know that?"

"I know you believe it was him, Miguel. But I swear to my God, it wasn't."

She crossed herself.

Miguel declared in disgust, "Ahhh! It was him—Frederick. That dog killed his own father."

Doris translated for Michael, as Isabel's timidity diminished with her rising emotions.

"Frederick is a good son," Isabel insisted. She knew she wasted words on Miguel and directed them to Doris. "He was lazy before and did nothing to help himself, but his father's death changed that. He has worked hard to make his father proud. I pray that in God's heaven there is a way for Señor Thomas to know this."

Doris listened sympathetically. She knew the woman had to get this out before being pressed on the subject of what else she heard that night.

"Miguel and I disagree, but time will show that Frederick is not an evil person." Isabel sighed. "I was awakened by voices that came from the main deck. It is two levels up from us, so I could not hear the words. But the voice, other than Señor Thomas's, was not Frederick Hawke."

Doris asked, "Did you recognize it?"

"It is one that I have heard before, but I can't recall who it belongs to."

"Could you make out any words?" Doris translated at Michael's request.

"I heard the voice of Señor Hawke when he said the words, 'you bastard'. I tell you, no man would call his own son a bastard. I heard scuffling then a splash alongside the boat."

Doris asked, "Why didn't you awaken Miguel?"

"I was frightened. I could tell Señor Hawke was angry. It is good to remain quiet and away from him when he gets like that. Miguel would have gotten up and gone to the main deck."

Miguel looked at her as though she betrayed him. "Señor Thomas was a kind man. He has given us everything we have, Isabel."

"He demanded much for what he gave. How many times did he strike me?"

Isabel became angry.

Miguel shouted, "No more than you deserved! He gave me … us a chance when there was nowhere else to turn."

Isabel disagreed. "Under him, it was worse for me than before I came to America. We did have a place to turn. We could have gone back."

Miguel looked at his wife through an expression bordering between anger and tenderness. Family meant everything to him. Thomas had been like a father, but like his own father, very abusive. And, like when he was a boy, Miguel believed it to be his own fault.

"Frederick paid us the wages his father owed," said Isabel. "This is how we could help Renaldo become a doctor."

The pride in Isabel's face warmed both Doris and Michael.

"And I believe we were owed nothing. Señor Frederick is trying to buy our silence," Miguel protested.

Isabel asked, "What is it he expects we know that we can be silent about?"

"The fact that we have told none of this to the Sheriff. The money is to ensure we do not do so."

Frederick's arrival interrupted the meeting, but Doris and Michael had gotten enough for later discussion.

He exclaimed, "Doris and Michael! What a nice surprise. Join me for one of Isabel's famous Margaritas and tell me of your day on the island."

Though Frederick had invited the four of them to share the plush shower facilities and bathing aboard Vega, Doris and Michael agreed to hold that luxury to themselves. Don't bite the hand that feeds, Michael reasoned. So with a pocketful of quarters, the kids, sweaty and grimy from the long bike ride, headed up the pier for the public showers.

Both quite hungry, they'd make short work of it. Michael would spring for dinner at the McMillin Restaurant expecting his son's customary appetite to be in perfect form. Tales of his dad's prime rib had Joseph salivating throughout the day.

Doris said, "They seem to get along."

She and Michael shared a Corona on *Vietvet's* main deck.

He replied, "Yeah, but more like a coupla Marine buddies than potential guy and girlfriend."

"I suspect that's mostly Liz. She took the divorce hard and blames my ex. I noticed a distinct change in her attitude toward men after that."

Michael suggested, "I'm sure that'll change when she meets the right guy."

"Right now she's up to her eyeballs in sports media. And persistent as she is, I'm sure she'll poke her head into that tent. Guess you've learned a lot about Joseph by now."

Her comment invited Michael to discuss his son, but she would not pursue it unless he wished to.

"Joseph makes me proud to be his father."

"No surprise. The apple doesn't fall far from the tree."

She gave him a tender look that made him happy with their developing relationship. Doris frequently signaled she had not closed the door on remarriage. Thoughts of a permanent arrangement appealed to Michael. He'd prefer marriage for a number of reasons, not least of all, it would be the most acceptable alternative on campus. He continued to struggle with the how and best timing for broaching this subject.

Returning to the topic of Joseph, he said, "Despite his apparent military bearing, I'm not sure about the Marine Corps for the long pull."

"Oh?"

"I would hate for him to think he has to do this for me. I'm not much on the chip off the old block syndrome. He should pursue the life he'll enjoy most."

"The little that I know of him, Joseph seems the kind of boy who will do just that."

Joseph, though no longer a boy, tended to remain so in the eyes of Doris.

"The other side of the coin: a lot of generals start off like Joseph. Are you familiar with the term gung ho?"

"No."

"It's a battle cry hangover from World War II. It symbolizes determination to overcome all obstacles, despite the enemy's strength. Simple rules are the easiest to follow. Most Marines like to come across as gung ho early in their careers and strive to achieve this. Others realize the times are changing, and what's been best for the Corps a few years ago, might not be today. The brighter ones tread more carefully, but at the risk of dirty looks from their peers. I think Joseph might be in that category. Time will tell."

"He's certainly his own man," said Doris, "and will definitely land on his feet."

"I'm greatly indebted to the Ungers. They've done well by him." Michael shifted in his seat to show he believed the topic had run its course and then changed it. "So, what did Nora Charles get out of the Vargas interviews?"

"Wow! Frederick arrived in the nick of time, didn't he? Do you think there was more they had to tell?"

"Don't know, really," he said. "But I'm beginning to believe my calibrations on both Frederick and his dad might be off the mark."

"I just can't feel comfortable around Frederick."

"If you believe Isabel, his father's death was the big turning point in Frederick's life. He's had only three years to change from a ne'er-do-well son to the image he now tries to project. Maybe he just tries too hard. This can make people look awfully stupid. You ought to give him the benefit of the doubt."

"Letting us use the bath facilities on his boat helps," she conceded.

With that, they headed off to *Vega* with toilet articles, towels and clothes planned for the evening. They needed no towels as these along with luxurious terry cloth robes were all provided by their thoughtful host. Frederick gained ground in Doris's perception.

People at tables nearby the one Michael reserved at the McMillin could easily get caught up in Liz's account of their afternoon event at Lime Kiln Lighthouse. It evoked a lot of laughter.

"Liz, you didn't," said Doris, but she could not contain her laughter.

Joseph said, "And I'm the last to find out. The most affected, but last to find out. So the old green-eyed monster finally caught up with Liz the cool."

"Over you? In your dreams, Picky!"

Michael asked, "Picky?"

"Yeah, Dad ... short for Confederate General George E. Pickett, per my jealous friend, here."

"Oh come off it, Picky. She was so blatantly obvious, I had to rescue you," Liz replied. "But when Picky mounted up to lead his troops against the Yankees, that poor girl's chin dropped almost to her knees."

Joseph declared, "These Washington girls. Never had such problems in California."

Liz exclaimed, "Lucky you!"

The sound of live music floated up from the Madrona Café. "Let's go, Picky. For a Marine, this guy dances pretty good."

The kids prepared to leave.

Sternly looking at her daughter, Doris said, "Liz."

Liz caught the meaning. "Oh, thank you for dinner, Michael. I loved it."

"Me too, Dad. It'll be a long time before I see a prime rib like that again."

Doris and Michael shook their heads as the kids departed, but shared expressions of admiration. Great rewards accrued to parenting, but none so much as when offspring seem to have found their way.

Their waiter approached.

Michael offered, "Would you like a Grand Marnier, Doris?"

Delighted he picked up on this so quickly, she replied. "Sure, Michael."

"Think I'll take a page out of the chief's book and have a cognac. Do you have any Remy Martin?"

"Of course, sir."

While they waited, Michael touched on their afternoon discussion with Miguel and his wife. "Thomas must have been a tough character, if you can believe Isabel."

"What's not to believe? I watched her body language and caught nothing but sincerity. If Isabel is acting, she's in the wrong business. She'd make a fortune in the movies."

"Then it adds Miguel to the suspect list. If Thomas abused him and his wife, he has motive."

"I don't think so for two reasons. One, woman's intuition. Miguel was apparently abused by his own father to the extent he believed it was part of life. All he had for Thomas was admiration and gratitude for lifting him from poverty."

"You said two reasons."

"Isabel was too light a sleeper to let Miguel leave her bed unnoticed."

Michael shook his head. "Nora Charles, eat your heart out."

From their window seat, they watched night descend upon the harbor.

"What a magnificent sight," he said. "You having a good time?"

"Do you have to ask?"

"I sure am." Michael thought a second and then decided to go with his feelings. "I always do when you're around."

She gave him a smile. "It's getting to be a two-way street."

"I haven't felt this way since I was a kid."

"I'm glad. We shouldn't let them have all the fun."

"They try to, that pair. Look, Doris—"

The waiter arrived with the drinks and interrupted Michael's question.

Doris correctly sensed it and answered. "I'm having a great time. I've gotten one of the answers we invited Liz for. She has no problems with you and me. That shouldn't be a factor, but for me, it is. Liz likes you, so consider Ralph Jr. a done deal. She wraps him around her little finger."

He reached across the table and took her hand. "And I buy into that. Joseph and I are just beginning our relationship, so I can't say I know how you feel."

She asked, "How do you feel about me?"

The question caught him totally off guard. *What an opening for the English Lit Prof,* he thought. But nothing from his repertoire jumped out. He wasn't good at this and would likely screw it up if he tried anything fancy.

Why not go with the simple facts? "How do I feel about you? Like I said before, it's good to be around you. When our time together is about to run out, I always want to make it last longer. When we say good-bye, the foremost thing on my mind is when I'll see you again. And when we're apart, the hardest thing for me is not to pick up the phone out of fear of making a pest of myself."

Doris squeezed his hand. "For an old Marine, that wasn't too shabby." She kissed him on the cheek. "No, Michael, that's not what I meant to say at all. Every woman should get to hear a man say that to her at least once in her life. Thank you for bringing it into mine. You're a keeper."

Michael heard the ship's clock strike two bells, 1:00 a.m. He fell back into a light sleep.

Shortly after, Joseph whispered, "Dad."

Michael slowly rousted himself. "What, Joseph?"

"I think somebody's come aboard. They're moving about topside."

Joseph kept his voice low.

Michael took a moment to clear his head. "Okay, tell me what you heard. I don't hear anything now."

"Be very quiet and listen," said Joseph. "Sounds like someone is working on something topside. And, Dad?"

"Yes?"

"Whoever it is didn't board from the dock. It was the starboard side. Has to be either a swimmer or someone with a boat."

"How do you know that?"

"Sound was over there, and I felt the boat list a bit to starboard. What could he possibly be screwing around with up there? And why?"

A number of things ran through Michael's mind. A hatch covered the main cabin where the women slept. *Could he be trying to pry that open? Could it be someone trying to frighten Doris and him out of investigating the Hawke case?*

"Okay, Joseph, let's think this thing through. He's putting himself too much at risk not to be armed."

"Do we have any weapons aboard?"

"A signal flare gun works at close range."

Michael retrieved it and installed a cartridge.

Liz yelled from the main cabin. "Picky, is that you up there?"

The intruder had to be alerted by that. "Let's get him, Dad!"

The two men raced onto the main deck hoping to at least identify the intruder before he escaped.

"Hold it right there, or I'll let you have it," ordered Michael as he brandished the flare gun.

The men looked forward at a large shape that reared up and made a terrible grunting sound. Downwind of the animal the powerful odor of raw fish overcame them as a huge sea lion waddled off the deck and into the water. The remains of a Dungeness crab rested on the forward deck. The sea lion crunching through its shell accounted for the suspicious noise.

Liz yelled again, "Picky! Who was that?"

The quick thinking Joseph replied, "Aliens. Twenty or so. But no match for the Marine Corps. They knew they were beat when Dad yelled *Semper Fi* at them."

Doris's steady voice demanded, "Michael, what's going on up there?"

"A visitor from the dark and murky depths. C'mon up and I'll explain."

The noise awakened the occupants of several nearby boats and a voice asked, "Everything okay over there?"

"Thank you," Michael replied. "A sea lion climbed aboard and surprised us. He's gone now."

Liz exclaimed, "Sea lion! You sure it wasn't a Yankee?"

Joseph quipped, "Maybe a Yankee Sea Lion."

Excitement abated about the dock; the old folks, as Liz called them, returned below to their bunks.

Liz and Joseph sat awhile. "Just to make sure he doesn't come back for the rest of his crab," she explained. Then after a quiet moment, "How come you don't say nice things to me, Picky? A perfect night at Roche Harbor, the sky full of stars, and all you do is sit there and twiddle your thumbs."

One thing Liz could be depended upon for: unpredictability. If a spark of interest existed in her, it evaded him completely.

"I don't want to open myself to a one-liner from the best comedienne since Lucille Ball."

"Am I really that bad?"

"Who said bad?"

Joseph thought a moment. Perhaps her antics at the lighthouse had really been to protect her interest in him. From all he'd seen so far, this would be welcome. "It's nice to have you around."

That ought to be safe enough. Wrong!

"It's nice to have you around? Wow, Picky. I'm swept right off my feet. How about beautiful, exciting? You know … all the things a guy's supposed to say to make a girl feel special."

"Promise I won't get another shot in the ribs?"

"You're special, Picky."

She looked up at him and he kissed her gently on the lips.

"How about we dance?"

He turned on the boom box loaded with Doris's romantic tunes by Frank Sinatra then set the volume low so as not to disturb the neighbors. He considered one surprise a night to be plenty. Barefoot, they put their arms about each other and swayed gently to the soft music.

"I was really scared, Picky. You don't mind if I call you that?"

"It's okay, Liz."

He liked to say her name, and enjoyed the feel of her body. He debated whether to tell her that. *Maybe it's too early.*

"I felt good about having you to protect me," she admitted, "even though it turned out to be only a sea lion."

"Twenty aliens," he corrected.

"Now look who can't be serious."

The Chairman floated through a moving treatment of *Strangers in the Night.*

"This is the right song," he said. "That's what we are, Liz, strangers in the night. But I intend to change that."

She looked up at Joseph and rewarded him with a smile. "Now that's more like it."

Chapter 6

Doris and Michael looked first at the coffee and toast they shared on the afterdeck of *Vietvet*, then at Liz and Joseph as they left at a brisk pace to breakfast at the Lime Kiln Café.

Michael said, "Ah, to be young again. Put away all those groceries and actually get thinner."

"That is a side of the coin," Doris agreed, "but being where I am right now has too many advantages."

"Think about what you're saying, Doris …eggs, sausage, sweet rolls, all in the background of a beautiful morning at Roche?"

"I've gotten far too comfortable with all the experience the years have given me. It makes life pleasant. Sometimes I can't believe the things I agonized over when I was Liz's age."

"Shaw was right? Youth is wasted on the young?"

Doris reasoned, "Not in the least. Young people need all that energy to deal with their perceptions of what life is all about. We don't have those problems."

"Just a second … I'll get my scratch pad and take a few notes. Maybe I'll teach philosophy next quarter."

Doris laughed. "Am I that profound?"

"Actually, you're right. But then when aren't you?"

Michael continued to be amazed by how much he discovered about women since Doris came into his life.

"On the subject of being right, what is it you're so fond of saying? *We're running out of daylight.* This time tomorrow, we'll be under way for Port Angeles; from what I can tell, we're a long way from unraveling the Thomas Hawke case."

"Like I just said, when aren't you right, Doris? I'm almost wishing we hadn't gone to Frederick's party Friday night. This is a great day for goofing off. Maybe instead of philosophy, I'll teach a new course this fall … Goofing Off I. Sound good?"

"No sympathy from me, Michael. You eat this up, and I must confess you got me enjoying it too. Where do we go from here?"

Thirty minutes later, they stood beside Roberta and Leo Walters' yacht, *Rebound.* The owners, not quite through their coffee on the fantail, immediately invited Doris and Michael aboard.

Roberta continued with her adulation of Michael's writing successes and made her pleasure over having them as guests quite obvious. Boaters are a hospitable sort. She disappeared to put on a fresh pot and left Leo to hold down the fort. After a few moments, Michael concluded his host not only conserved words, but syllables as well. Fortunately, the bubbling Roberta returned and reignited the conversation.

Her explanation of their boat's name origin did not surprise Michael. "Ten years ago, when Leo watched the NBA Championship game with a couple of friends, he said only one word during the entire second half ... *Rebound.* So, when we bought the boat the following year, it was a natural."

Michael broke the ice. He explained the request made of him by Miguel Vargas to look into the death of Thomas Hawke. He explained also the list given him by Ben Schulz.

"We're making the rounds and wondered if you folks can tell us anything on the subject."

Roberta looked at her husband, who emerged abruptly from one syllable land.

Anger flashed in Leo's eyes as he said, "If there was a single tear shed at his funeral, I sure as hell didn't see it."

Doris jumped in. "We're finding this pretty much the case with the others. Would you share your reasons?"

Roberta looked frightened, but said nothing.

Leo snapped, "You're damn right I'll tell you. Thomas Hawke was a son of a bitch of the first water. He had nothing but contempt for all of the people on Schulz's list. You know, we all lived near the Hawke place in Eastern Washington.

Farmers, like him, until he gobbled us up and it didn't hurt him one bit. Matter of fact, he enjoyed watching us squirm."

Leo sat quiet only when he had no agenda.

Roberta said, "But he's gone, now, Leo. It's all in the past."

"My family had that farm for two generations. Every picture in the family album was taken there and that bastard, Hawke, converted the place into migrant worker quarters."

"The migrants are good people," Roberta said.

"Right! And they deserved a helluva lot better than the tenement he made of that fine old house."

Doris quieted their rising emotions. "What can you tell us about how all this started?"

Leo looked off into the harbor to compose himself. "It began three years ago, in the winter of ninety-two. Peter Bushnell, his buddy the chief, and me met at Bushnell's place to compare notes on the way things went for us the previous year."

The windows of the Bushnell home in central Washington rattled from a stiff winter wind that drifted snow up on the driveway. The three men sat about the living room fireplace at mid evening, sipping cups of hot coffee. Seriousness of their agenda precluded customary bourbons.

Leo said, "Damn, Peter, that last gust sounded like it could take off the chimney."

The chief agreed. "If we don't get a move on, we'll be snowed in here."

Peter replied, "We've got plenty of room."

Leo just enjoyed one of Etta Bushnell's superb dinners and thoughts of breakfast here appealed to him.

Peter said, "Think it's too late already. You two are stuck here till the plow goes through in the morning, so you might as well make yourselves comfortable."

Neither man said anything. Their silence conceded Peter's logic.

Leo said, "Peter, I'm not sure how many more seasons I got left in me. Maybe only one if it doesn't come in better than last year."

The chief's eyes turned toward his boss.

Peter replied, "That's a familiar tune around here. The cost of everything except fruit and produce continues to go up."

"I'd kinda like to wrap it up soon," said Leo. "But I don't want to leave my boys with a dying turkey. Seems like there ought to be something I can do. Old Hawke does okay. Maybe he could give us a few steers."

Peter looked at his friend. "That summer place of yours in Port Ludlow beckons to become year around? Can't say I blame you. When you go, I'll have to lock the chief up to keep him from going with you. Problem is you'd never get him off the *Rebound*. That's one helluva boat you got there."

Leo said, "Yeah, but I'd enjoy it a lot more if I knew the farm wasn't in such damn trouble. I can't figure out how Hawke does it. Sure, greater volume than us, but that means more labor, fertilizer and taxes. When I add up everything, it doesn't account for how much he can undersell us."

The chief looked on in silence. The management end of farming did not suit him. But if you want to go somewhere in a boat, find someone like him to go with you. Peter kept him on mainly for that reason. That and the fact the chief's Navy retirement enabled him to work for a lot less.

Leo continued. "The total acreage of our two farms exceeds his. Maybe if we combined?"

"Problem there is that Thomas's profit goes only to him. Ours would be divided two ways."

Leo asked, "Think he has income from anywhere else?"

"Could have a still and run a moonshine operation. But if it's within a hundred miles of here, the chief would smell it out, right?" Peter wished to change the subject. "Chief, tell them about how you used to filter torpedo alcohol through a loaf of bread to make it drinkable. What was it you called that stuff?"

"Pink Lady," the chief replied. "The stuff they added to keep us from drinking it made it pink. Took the government years to figure out how to do this, and us only a month to learn how to fix it."

The serious talk over, and no need for anyone to drive home, Peter Bushnell replaced coffee with a more serious libation.

The following morning, all three, after a well fed breakfast by Etta, climbed into Leo's pickup and headed off to the Hawke farm. The morning broke bright and clear and a brisk northwest wind signaled passing of a weather front that moved the storm eastward into the Rockies. Eastern Washington and Idaho now shared the benefits.

Leo asked, "So, old Thomas wasn't troubled by our wanting to see him. You tell him the subject?"

"In general," Peter replied. "He didn't seem too eager, but then he never does."

The chief, jammed into the middle and sucking on the last of his coffee, remained his usual silent self.

Leo would not abandon his gut feel. "I still believe Thomas has something else going. Otherwise, he's gotta be taking a beating like the rest of us."

Peter suggested, "Maybe we'll find out today."

A few moments later, they pulled up the long drive to the most prosperous spread in the county. The traditional white frame farmhouse had been replaced by a mansion-like structure surrounded by outbuildings that resembled an industrial complex rather than a farmyard.

Miguel Vargas greeted them at the door and showed them to a well-appointed office. "Señor Hawke will join you shortly. Would you like coffee?"

All accepted and Miguel disappeared.

The chief made a rare comment. "When I look at Miguel, I see a terrified man."

Peter replied, "Well, if anyone can recognize terror, it's you, Chief. Seen a lot of it during the war, I guess?"

"Prefer the stuff I saw in the war to the kind Miguel has. We knew the war would end, but I don't know about Miguel."

Speculation on Miguel's plight ended with the arrival of Thomas, of whom the chief once said, "He don't even dress like a farmer."

The three wore flannel plaid shirts, jeans, or khaki trousers. Hawke arrived in gray slacks, white shirt, navy blazer and an ascot.

The chief thought, *If that don't beat everything.*

"Good morning, gentlemen. Miguel will bring us coffee in a moment. Would you like anything else? Sweet rolls, perhaps?" He shook each man's hand and spoke their names, ending with, "Ah, Chief. What color you bring to our little valley."

Stanley Porter saw the put-down. It translated to, *What's a jackass like you doing in a business meeting?*

But the chief had thick skin and took the dig in stride. He reasoned, *the son of a bitch is trying to make me mad. If I do, he wins and that ain't gonna happen.* The chief's years grew short and he wasted little time doing other than what he wanted. He'd leave, but not before he got some coffee.

Thomas asked, "So, what can I do for you this beautiful morning?"

Peter took the lead, and explained their concerns, then added, "We hoped you might have some pointers for us. If things keep going the way they are, we won't make it through another year."

"Cut your costs to lower produce costs and be competitive," Thomas explained simply. He could imply a sneer through an expression most would consider compassionate.

Peter replied for the three. "A lot easier said than done, Thomas. We hoped you'd have a few suggestions for us. We don't see any obvious differences between your operation and ours, yet you beat us at market every time."

"Does Macy's tell Gimbels? Competition, my friends, the backbone of free enterprise. It is good for the country and ultimately for the consumer."

"Agree completely. We must get our stuff out at your prices or nobody will buy it. If we do that, we're left with not enough margin to even pay taxes. We'd like to know how you're able to meet expenses, much less turn the obvious profit that you do. Or, at least give us some clues."

"Isn't it rather simple? With the market set, you've got to limit what you pay for supplies and labor."

All of us pay minimum wage, and I know for a fact Hawke's labor per acre is the same as ours, thought Leo, *so that part's a red herring.*

Miguel interrupted the meeting with a steaming pot of coffee, cups, cream, sugar and a tray of sweet rolls.

Recalling Hawke's earlier snide remark, the chief surmised Thomas did not want him around for the meeting. He took a cup of coffee and sweet roll then excused himself to go outside for a smoke.

"We promise not to discuss anything of significance until you return, Chief." This time Thomas did not mask the sneer. Feigning seriousness about his promise to the chief, Thomas changed the subject. "It is no surprise we're all boaters. What better way to take a respite from farming than the sea. And even you, Peter, have joined our ranks. A sailboat, yes, but at least something to get you out on the water." No one could stick in a barb quite like Thomas.

Peter responded with, "The Ranger's a lot of fun. And I don't think I could get the chief out on anything else. He claims the Navy gave him enough power boating to last a lifetime."

"Do you think the chief can find Roche Harbor?"

Peter made light of Thomas's second barb. "If it's up there, he will."

"Good. What do you think of an annual neighborhood rendezvous at Roche, in say, late August or early September? It would be my pleasure to host cocktails and dinner aboard the

Vega. And the rest of the weekend we can have some well deserved play time."

Leo and Peter exchanged glances.

"Just a suggestion, gentlemen. Strikes me the timing is right for getting out of here to kick up our heels. What do you think of the idea?"

"Well, Roberta for one would vote yes."

"Etta too. She hates to sail, but loves the parties at the places we stop. She'd likely arrive by ferry, but that's okay."

Thomas asked, "Maybe take care of a little business while we're up there?"

Peter replied, "Why not?"

Thomas's son, Frederick, entered the office. "You all know Frederick?"

"Good morning Leo, Peter. Father, may I have a word with you?"

"Seems the storm kept Frederick home last night, and he'll need some sustenance to take up where he left off in Seattle. Excuse us, please, gentlemen."

The pair disappeared to another part of the house.

Peter and Leo could hear Thomas's raised voice but could not make out the words, other than they weren't pleasant.

"Wow," said Peter. "What a bastard."

Leo said, "What else is new? But he's the only game in town."

When Thomas returned the two thanked him for his hospitality, excused themselves and offered to show themselves out. Thomas would not hear of it and summoned Miguel to perform this *honor.*

On reaching the door, they could not spot the chief. They looked about and called him.

Soon Porter, with his distinctive gate, came from the backside of the house. "Took a little walk," he explained. "There was more bullshit in Thomas's office than the whole damn barnyard."

The two laughed their agreement.

Leo asked, "I wonder if his game is to squeeze us out. And when we're gone, buy up our places for a song. Maybe he's not making a dime more than us, but has the capital to last us out?"

Peter Bushnell nodded. "You got a point, Leo."

A light swell gently rolled the *Rebound* as Michael's wrist began to ache from rapid-fire notes he had taken. "Well, that's sure an earful."

Doris focused on Roberta throughout the conversation. She seemed quite nervous. *Perhaps a private talk later in the day will net something.*

Roberta asked, "Where's Liz and Joseph?"

Michael replied, "Probably back on the boat by now." He explained the reason for separate breakfasts.

Leo asked, "Dieting good for both body and soul?"

Doris replied, "Very good."

"You think the kids would like to check my crab pots? Best way of eating fresh Dungeness at Roche."

"My guess is yes. Liz has never done that, which means she'll want to."

They made their apologies, expressed their thanks and prepared to leave.

"Just have the kids drop by then I'll set them up with the dinghy and show them how to find the pots."

As they walked down the dock, Doris asked, "Who's next?"

"On the heels of what we just heard, your favorite."

"The chief?"

"Right, but let's be sure to talk to him away from Peter. I want that conversation to be separate."

Chapter 7

Joseph made no attempt to remain cool when Liz emerged from below decks in a red bikini.

She read his expression like an open book. "I need to work on my tan," Liz defended.

"You wanna make all the little boats run into each other out there?"

They headed for Leo Walters' yacht to take the dinghy out to check crab pots.

"Will this make you run into somebody, Picky? I thought you were the big Annapolis navigator."

Joseph smiled in response and continued to look at her.

"Can't you look someplace else? You're making me self-conscious."

"You got on the wrong outfit to get guys to look somewhere else."

"Well, at least you're good for my ego, Picky."

Liz's shapely and slender body turned heads as they walked down the dock and earned a double take from the normally dour Leo when they arrived.

Leo pointed out an area across the harbor where a group of crab pot buoys dotted the waters with colorful markers. "Three of those are mine, red and white. You'll be able to tell because my name's on them." Leo explained how to bait the traps, catch limits, and minimum size, but told Joseph not to worry. "I only keep the ones big enough to satisfy one person at a single sitting. That's four of you, and I'm sure the harbor will be generous."

Liz declined to don the life vest. "Not good for the tan line, and it's softer than the bench." She placed it there and sat on it. "Well, fire this thing up, Picky, and let's get going. I want to catch a few of those little devils. Ever do this before?"

"Everybody whoever crabbed had to do it for the first time. This is mine."

The outboard motor sputtered to life with a first pull on the start cord, and they putt-putted away from the *Rebound.*

"Don't go near any boats, Picky. I don't want to cause any accidents."

"Maybe we should notify the Coast Guard."

Clear of the piers, Joseph sped them out into a glorious morning, Liz's ponytail waving in the bright sunlight.

They reached the buoys and quickly found Leo's crab pots. The first produced three, eight to nine inches across the back. Joseph, handled these per Leo's instructions; grab them at a place out of reach of their claws, then deposit them into the ice chest.

"That's cool, Picky. Trick is if your cooking is good as your catching."

Joseph gave his best imitation of a Native American voice, "Brave hunt, squaw cook and walks behind brave's horse while he rides."

"You do all this and tell fairy tales at the same time. Not bad, Picky."

Emptying the second pot created a problem. It held six … two big and four little ones. Separating them shattered Joseph's great white hunter image. The first big one made it into the cooler. The second missed and tottered on the gunwale, then fell back into the boat and made a beeline for Liz.

She stood up and shouted, "Picky … do something!"

Joseph couldn't reach the crab. He stood in a jerky motion that listed the boat enough to topple Liz into the drink with an unceremonious splash. She reappeared above the surface.

"Get those damn things out of the boat, Picky. I'm freezing!"

He grabbed the crab and tossed it over the side.

"Not here by me. He'll come after me again."

"It's that bathing suit. He's probably a guy crab."

"Don't be a smart-ass, Picky, and get me back in the boat."

Joseph laughed so hard, he almost couldn't get her out of the water. With some effort, he succeeded.

Her teeth chattering, she folded her arms about herself.

Joseph quickly removed his T-shirt. "Here, it'll screw up your tan, but you better put it on. First, use it like a towel and dry yourself off. The water on your skin is evaporating and it makes you cold. The sun will heat you up in no time."

Several smart remarks came to mind but Liz withheld them. The furrow in his brow showed genuine concern for her and she liked that. Liz did as Joseph instructed then donned the T-shirt.

She cupped his face with her hand. "You're sweet," she said then bussed him softly on the lips. Afterward, she realized she couldn't handle the appreciative expression on Joseph's face. Feeling the tender moment awkward, she cut it short. "I thought Marines are supposed to protect us private citizens."

Joseph grinned at her then hauled up the third trap. "I'll try to be a little more careful. Maybe we'll luck out and they'll all be chicks."

He culled out three for the cooler, re-baited the pot and returned it to the water. They made a circuit of the harbor to admire the splendid watercraft moored there then motored back alongside *Vietvet* to deliver their epicurean treasures.

Stanley Porter, aka the chief, shivered on the veranda of Thomas Hawke's mansion-like farmhouse. He had second thoughts about being out here for his smoke. The house faced northwest, into the teeth of a twenty knot wind. Wind chill had to be well below zero. *But better here*, he thought. *The bullshit in Hawke's office has to be hip deep by now.*

During World War II in the southwest Pacific, he would frequently get permission to come to the submarine bridge for a smoke. The officer of the deck welcomed visitors, for each one represented an additional pair of eyes to look out for marauding aircraft. Everyone had a stake in the outcome, hence there never could be enough eyes on the bridge. Only exceptional vigilance assured survival. The chief always sought the leeward

side of the conning tower fairwater, out of the wind, and if the
sun happened to be shining on that side, so much the better.

A bright sun shone on the leeward side of Hawke's mansion
that morning. The chief raised his collar against the wind and
waded through snowdrifts headed in that direction. There, he
sat upon the back steps that had been cleared of snow. He felt
the cold boards through the seat of his jeans but body heat soon
took care of that. He attributed this to lingering effects of
several of Peter Bushnell's cognacs he consumed the previous
evening. With the entire Hawke mansion for a windscreen and
the sun warming him, the chief reposed in the epitome of
comfort considering the cold morning.

He bore his sixty-five years well. Several *dodged bullets*
left him in need of looking after himself.

When complimented on how well he looked, he replied
always, "I can't afford to look any other way."

Cigarettes and cognac, his main vices, comprised the
greatest threat to his health. He was determined to kick the
former, but not the cognac; his view … *worse things than dying
can happen to a man.* Giving up his favorite alcoholic beverage
numbered among these.

The chief studied the elaborate complex of buildings on the
Hawke spread. Subconsciously, he attempted to discern their
function. He wondered if perhaps here lay the key to Thomas
Hawke's success story. Hawke, a relative newcomer in the
area, had been here only ten years compared with neighboring
orchards owned by incumbents for two or more generations.

The harsh voice of a man who had slipped up behind him
interrupted the chief's thoughts. "What are you doing here?"

The chief surmised the reason for the man's appearance
accumulated to the arrival of a rental panel truck, now backed
up to the largest of the outbuildings. Several men emerged and
spread out in the manner by which an armored car delivery
would be covered at a bank.

Looking the man over, the chief replied in an unperturbed voice, "Ducking the wind and having a smoke. What's it look like?"

The man, big and powerfully built, scowled a warning, "Take your goddamn smoke around to the other side of the house. Mr. Hawke know you're here?"

"Look, neighbor, I don't know what's eating you. I'll go back in the house when I'm finished with this smoke. You don't like it, call Thomas out here."

Use of Hawke's first name worked.

"Don't light up another one," the man said and walked off toward the truck.

The chief's capacity amazed Michael. Not quite 10:00 a.m. and already a crushed Bud Light can lay on the deck with a half empty one in his hand.

"So you never saw what came out of the truck? Any ideas?"

"Nope. That was Hawke's business. This fella was big, tough and made it clear he didn't want me around. Mrs. Porter didn't raise no fools."

Doris tried the charm approach by putting her hand softly on his arm. "That must have been scary."

"Nope. The click-click of a depth charge about to go off is scary. That goon might've beaten me up but could never scare me away."

Michael asked, "If you had to make a guess, Chief, what do you think might have been in that truck you saw at the Hawke place? You know, after old Thomas tossed you out of the meeting."

"Dunno. But whatever it was probably made Hawke's spread pay off."

"You never went back to check?"

"Like I said, Mrs. Porter didn't raise no fools."

Michael thanked the chief and asked him to let Peter Bushnell know they came by.

"Yep," said the Chief.

Michael wondered. Every time he dropped by Bushnell's Ranger, he found only the chief. *Where's Peter, and what could he be doing? Roche is too small to get lost in.*

Doris asked, "So where to now, Michael?"

"The list provider, Ben Schultz."

The two walked off down the pier. The chief's streaky gray eyes followed them until they disappeared from sight.

Liz continued to work on her tan, but this time in white shorts and a blue tank top, her bikini spread out on the main cabin roof to dry in the sun. They shared what remained of the morning coffee, and Joseph attacked a sweet roll.

"You're a bottomless pit, Joseph. Do all Marines eat that much?"

"I'm thinking of becoming a Recon Marine. Off on our own a lot so we have to forage. You know, eat when we find it because we travel light with no room for rations."

"I'm just not gonna win, am I?"

"You always win, Liz. Look at the way you got me all to yourself in spite of the lighthouse girl."

"Got you?! Rescued you. She was about to have you for lunch, but old Liz saved your bacon. Not like you did when the crabs attacked me."

"Don't know a lot about women, but enough not to go there. If that's the way you see it, I see it that way too."

"Sissy quitter."

"Bingo, Liz. You got me dead to rights."

A middle-aged man walked by with a West Highland Terrier on a leash. A few yards down the pier, a pair of young women stopped him to make a fuss over the dog, its wagging tail showing pleasure at the attention.

"See, Liz. I should do that. Get myself a boat and a little dog. Bring them here to Roche and let the chicks fall all over me."

"They're falling all over the dog, Twit. Not the guy."

"It's like fishing, Liz. The dog is the bait on the other end of the line. The chicks take it in and all he's gotta to do is reel them in."

She enjoyed a good laugh from Joseph's analogy. He had a quick mind and good with a comeback, a necessary quality to survive with Liz.

"Liz, I told you early this morning I intend to change us from being strangers in the night. Why don't you tell me something about you?"

"What's to tell?"

"An original line if I ever heard one. But I guess you need a starting point. Tell me about when you were little ... brothers and sisters. I'm an only child and missed having siblings."

"I was born and raised in Bellevue, Washington, and I've got a truly cool kid brother, Ralphie."

"What's he doing now?"

"He'll be a senior at the University of Colorado—an architect major and linebacker on the football team. Right now, he's at Bellevue with Dad and his stepmom."

"He's got to be pretty good to play with the Buffaloes."

"My fault. He was two years behind me in high school and had to measure up to his big sister. I played them all ... volleyball, track, basketball, softball, you name it. Everyone expected the same of him so he did his best."

"You were varsity?"

"Yep. Only volleyball in college. A little short, but one helluva setter."

"You guys must be close? You and Ralphie."

"Like ham and eggs. When I went off to the U, it wasn't all that far from Bellevue so I saw a lot of him. Mom and I tried to see as many of his high school games as possible. When he went off to college, I learned just how close we were. I really miss him."

"Ralphie's a lucky guy."

"Ralph to you. I'm the only one who gets away with Ralphie."

"Like Picky?"

"I guess. I'm probably being set up for a fish-in, but why do you think he's lucky."

"To have a sister like you. That would've been really neat."

For a fleeting moment, it occurred to Liz that's what accounted for Joseph's attraction to her, need of a sibling. Then she recalled his expression on seeing her in the bikini, not a look brothers give to sisters. She gave Joseph a rare smile.

"That's nice, Picky."

"You mind talking about why your mom and dad split?"

"No. It was rough, but I handle it pretty well now. Dad's a neat guy. A real success story on Bellevue's *doctors avenue*, 116th Street. I think he regrets breaking up the marriage. It was his doing. Midlife crisis, I think they call it. Sure you want to hear this?"

"Only if you want to tell me."

He regarded her through an expression of true interest.

She reflected an instant. Little as she knew about Joseph, he did not seem the kind of person who took pleasure in listening to sad stories. She found herself strangely pleased at having made such a friend. *A good person to vent on.* In Liz's unpredictable life, there could not be too many of those.

"It was ten years ago. Dad's practice preoccupied him to the point he never had time for us. Mom took care of everything, including vacations, school, trips back east to visit the grandparents, and the like. She blames herself. Dad apparently expected her to drop everything and tend his needs. After all, looking after sick people was a noble thing to do. Why couldn't Mom see that?"

Liz's anger grew as she recalled these unhappy events, her usual flippant approach to life nowhere in sight.

He looked into her eyes and said in a steady voice, "You don't have to talk about this if you don't feel like it, Liz. I just want to know a little something about you."

"This is about me," she replied. "Don't get me wrong. Dad is a great father to me. If anything, he spoils the hell out of both

Ralphie and me. He bends over backwards to respect me as a woman and has honored my privacy since I was a little girl. He was stern but always reasonable. I've never known him to do anything that was not in my best interest, that is before the divorce. He taught me to be particular in choosing a man ... he should show me the same respect that Dad does. Well dammit, Picky, why couldn't he respect Mom like he did me? She deserved it a lot more than I did."

She put her hands to her face and burst into tears.

This made Joseph feel awkward. He didn't handle this sort of thing well. He pulled his chair closer to hers and took her hands in his.

"I'm sorry, Liz. I didn't mean—"

"It's okay," Liz said in a recomposed voice. "I want to finish."

He gave her hand a gentle squeeze.

"All Mom did was do what she believed was right for Ralphie and me. While we were out of town, Claire, the woman who ran the office, gave Dad the sympathy and understanding he believed Mom withheld from him. I'm not all that sure that was Claire's sole motive. Marrying Dad took her instantly from a struggling single Mom to a prosperous Bellevue matron."

"A lot of people get divorced. My Dad, for example."

"I know about that. Mom told me. There was never really a marriage. Your birth mother canned your dad when he was in Vietnam and let you go at birth." Liz put a hand to her mouth. "I'm sorry, Picky. Are you close to your birth mother?"

"Saw her for the first time a month ago. She's the exact opposite of Dad. Spent most of the visit telling me how sorry she was for what happened. I sensed she said this only to ease her conscience. Never said a word about seeing me again. Not like Dad. Never in my life have I known someone so overjoyed at just being with me."

"I like him, Picky. I hope Mom marries him."

Joseph believed his dad and Doris remained in the wait and see mode, but did not share this.

"It's the only way Mom will let my dad out of her life. She loved him so much, Picky. It was so tough for her. Ralphie and I were furious, but even in her pain she told us if we loved Dad, we should let him do what makes him happy. But he's gone forever to our mom. She realizes that, but until someone else comes along, she'll never let go. She needs someone else to give her love to and fuss over. I truly believe, Michael, your dad is the guy."

"Thanks for saying that. I'm surprised how well you know him in such a short while. Your mom is great. Certainly has been very nice to me."

Joseph struggled with words, and Liz took pity.

"I've had a lot more time with Mom than you've had with your dad. She's told me a great deal about him. She seems a lot happier since Michael came into the picture. I hope it continues."

"How did your brother deal with the divorce?"

"Not very well. He was only in eighth grade. He loved Dad with a passion and couldn't handle the trauma of knowing Dad had betrayed Mom. The divorce decision devastated him. It was like he discovered everything he believed in was a lie and wanted to strike back at Dad. He stole a car and was arrested for driving it under the influence. If it weren't for Dad's connections and some damn big attorney fees, it would have been juvenile detention."

"Not a very happy time for you."

Joseph continued to be at a loss for words but knew Liz wanted to continue.

"Fortunately, Ralphie confided in me with everything. Mom asked me to let him move in for a few weeks in the apartment Dad got me in the U-District for school. The breakup was at its peak and our home was no place for Ralphie just then. God love her, she drove him to and from high school every day in rush hour traffic both ways."

"He turned out okay then? I guess so with college and everything."

"You two guys would hit it off," Liz declared. Then went on, "It had nothing to do with the divorce, but Dad's practice really took off afterwards. I know Mom wonders if she was holding him back, but there's not a word of truth in that. Mom did okay with her settlement, but she lost what she wanted most, Dad. Claire is in control of everything now and would not let Dad go under any circumstance. It's way too good a deal for her."

"Your mom seems like the kind of lady who wouldn't go back regardless of what becomes of your dad."

"No. It would be another wrong. Mom says two wrongs don't make a right. Look, Picky, I don't mean that if things work out for Mom and your dad that he will be second best. Mom was hurt, but mainly because the man she trusted did her dirt. Maybe she was hurt more by herself for being dumb enough to believe in Dad through all those years."

"I don't believe that, Liz. Your mom has quality written all over her."

"There's a big downside to this for me, Picky. Dad was my idol. He showed me a standard I should measure every man to. But he wasn't truthful. How will I know this about a man until he dumps me? Like Dad dumped Mom."

She set her jaw. A tear appeared, but she blinked it back. She glared at Joseph through her anger as though she expected him to explain this.

"If I had that answer, Liz, I'd be getting paid a lot more than a Marine Corps second lieutenant. My adoptive mom loved me, make no mistake about that, but it was tough love. She told me some of my decisions are going to be wrong, but the only thing worse than a bad decision is no decision at all. This sounds callous, Liz, but when the time comes, all you can do is pay your money and take your chances. My gut tells me you'll do okay. You've got a fabulous insight into people."

"Thanks for listening, Picky. You're a good head. You know that?"

"No, Liz, but I've learned if you say so, that's what it is."

"Am I that bad?"

"Actually, you're terrific. But one thing."

"Shoot." She gave him a puzzled look.

"Take the name Picky. You and I know where it comes from, but consider someone who hears it for the first time. Am I a picky guy or what?"

"So?"

"Can it be just between you and me?"

She grinned at him. "Not a chance, Picky."

He shrugged his shoulders. "Guess I gotta pick one for you."

"Liz works just fine, now this stranger in the night thing. What about you?"

"Where do I start?"

"Try the beginning. You know, Picky, I'm starting to wonder about my taxes. They teach you anything about that at Annapolis?"

"A guy doesn't have to worry about not being humble around you, Liz. Okay. You asked for it. I was raised in California. San Luis Obispo. You know I was adopted. My parents told me this when I was fairly young. Grew up with knowing that, and it didn't bother me a bit. My life was happy, but routine. I mean no big events like yours."

"Lucky you."

"I know that, Liz. Mom kept me on the straight and narrow. Had the feeling if she let up on me one little bit, she'd lose control. But I always felt loved by her. I know, because it was Mom who kept me from seeing my birth parents. She feared there was a chance they could take me back and she'd lose me."

"So you never saw Michael till a few months ago?"

"For all practical purposes. He came by to see me when I was eleven, but my adoptive dad introduced him only as an old friend. Michael was in his Marine uniform, and boy, was I impressed. Maybe that's how the seed got planted."

Liz asked, "Did you have any feelings there was something special about him?"

"No, but I instantly liked him. That was unusual for me, so maybe there was a connection I didn't pick up on."

"So what about high school. Any sports?"

"Only intramural, but I was editor for the school paper."

"You got that from your dad."

"I suppose. It was my adoptive dad who convinced Mom I should be given the opportunity to visit my birth parents. They gave me what I needed to find them during Graduation Week at Annapolis. With my commission in the Marine Corps, my adoptive parents knew how proud that would make Michael and could not deny him that."

"You like Michael a great deal, don't you, Picky?"

"Strange as it might sound, love would be more accurate, even though we've known each other for such a short time."

"It's not strange at all. Michael is a class person."

"Liz, this might sound dumb, but I'm gonna tell you anyway. Mom withheld her affection, even though I always sensed she was bursting to let it out. I think she considered it a sign of weakness, and I might use it as a lever against her to get my own way. My best buddy's mom had this habit of cupping his cheek for good-byes and the like. I envied him that. This morning on the crab boat when you did that, it made me feel great."

Liz's humor crutch evaded her and she cast about for other words of escape. She wished not to let herself be touched by this young man. Far too many things went on in her life right now to let a significant guy matter. Tomorrow, he'd be gone to who knows where, and when, if ever, would he return? *Don't say anything dumb,* she counseled herself.

"Thank you for being my friend." *That should be safe.*

"Wow," he replied, "look at us. Known each other less than forty-eight hours and look at the ground we've covered."

"No more strangers in the night?" she asked.

"No more strangers in the night," Joseph repeated.

Chapter 8

Doris set her jaw and did not turn to Michael when she spoke. "The chief knows more than he's telling us."

Michael paused for an instant and wished he hadn't let them become involved in what Doris now termed their *case*. He considered it a far too beautiful day to pass attempting to solve a crime that possibly had not even been committed, and this time tomorrow they'd be in Port Angeles, their port visit to Roche at an end.

Worse, the precious little time he had with Joseph slipped away too quickly. A late August sun spilled its warm rays upon them. Boards on the floating dock creaked underfoot as they walked past the many well-appointed pleasure craft. Just two weeks till the onset of the September to May *rain festival*; he could think of better ways to pass these final pleasant hours.

He wondered, *Could it be old age makes its mark on Harry Steele?* He, Doris and *kids* gave Michael the sense of family that had evaded him most of his life.

He'd have preferred to do other things, but acquiesced to her comment and asked, "Woman's intuition?"

"That, plus the chief's avoidance of eye contact. Not like him at all."

Michael cast his eyes about as they continued their walk. It seemed that everyone but him, preoccupied themselves with having a good time. He looked at his watch.

"It's eleven," he said. "Better head on over to the Lime Kiln. Can't have the kids fainting from hunger."

Doris asked, "Should we stop by the boat for Liz and Picky."

Joseph's new nickname had gained a foothold.

"A coupla eating machines like them? Bet they're already at the Kiln holding us a place in line."

They arrived and validated Michael's notion.

Michael and Joseph took lunch orders from the ladies, while Doris found an empty table.

Seated with her daughter for a few rare private moments, Doris began what mothers normally do, probe. "So what do you think of Joseph?"

Liz resorted to what daughters do best, reveal not a crumb more than she wanted her mom to know. "What's to think?"

"Oh you know what I'm talking about. He's a nice looking boy."

"I guess."

It would be like pulling teeth, but Doris the *dentist* persisted. "I could always tell when you were interested in a boy, because you'd tell me as little about him as you could possibly get away with."

"Mom!"

"If it looks like a duck, walks like a duck, quacks like a duck, chances are it's a duck."

Liz gave her favorite exasperated expression. "He's a nice guy, Mom. The kind you'd like me to hang out with. A world's champion rules obeyer. My guess is he even closes cover before striking, but Picky doesn't smoke, so I haven't seen him strike a match."

"Is he a good dancer?"

Liz knew her daughter's passion for dancing.

"He's a Marine, Mom. He's used to marching to music, so I guess dancing is not that far out of line for him."

Relentless, Doris pushed the envelope. "Having a good time?"

Liz knew her mom's bulldog tenacity could not be easily overcome. *All I got to do is stall her off till the guys get back.* She looked at the line and reckoned that would be at least another ten minutes. *Mom can get enough material for a full-length novel in that much time. Damage control. Say a lot without telling her anything*

"So, what do you talk about?"

The question gave Liz a point of defense. *Not a damn word about the Strangers in the Night talk.*

"Oh, he likes outdoor things. We biked yesterday and picked up crab pots today." *Tell her what she already knows.* "You surely talk to each other. What do you say?"

"Mom! Do I have to remind you we've only known each other for two days? And we're in a sort of forced situation here."

"Forced? Weren't you the one planning to pass the weekend studying in my apartment until you saw Joseph and his dad walking down the dock in Port Angeles?"

Liz saw through her mom's familiar irritation ploy. Get her daughter's back up and all kinds of things come blurting out.

Determined to be cool, she resisted the urge to say 'Nice try, Mom.' Instead Liz opted for the innocuous route. "He's a neat guy. Probably the most courteous boy I've ever hung out with. No surprise. Don't they teach them that at Annapolis?"

Doris, like the needle on an old thirty-three and a third record player, did not leave the groove. "You must talk about something."

Liz rolled her eyes. "He tells me about being in the Marine Corps." *No, that's not fair,* she thought. *Picky certainly doesn't bore me.* "Actually, Mom, he asks a lot about me. Where I was born, high school, college, what I like to do."

"Your sports?"

Liz replied, "Of course, Mom."

"Is he impressed?"

"Like I said, he's very polite." Liz cast an eye at the line and found the men had disappeared into the café. *Just stall a little longer.*

"Isn't that refreshing after the other guys you've hung out with? Take *I* and *me* from their vocabularies and they'd be speechless."

"Mom, you want to know if Picky and I are going anyplace? That's ridiculous. As I said, we've only known each other for two days. But if you want to know what I think …"

Doris had gotten her going, but withheld the smug look.

"He's a nice person, but we're like night and day. Picky's up to his neck in the Marine Corps. You'd not believe all the training they've got lined up for him."

"Where will he be stationed?"

"Camp Pendleton in California."

"That's not what I'd call off the end of the earth. And I'm sure he'll be up this way to see Michael."

"We made no plans to see each other. Why are you trying to make something out of nothing, Mom? I'm up to my buns in getting ready for sports media. You know that. Picky and I both are too busy with other things."

Doris nodded and thought, *The lady doth protest too much, methinks.* She'd find out what happened on Joseph's side without saying a word. Just watch the expression on his face when her daughter spoke. She had not long to wait. When the men returned, Joseph placed Liz's lunch before her like a waiter seeking a big tip. Their exchange of smiles revealed far more to the intuitive Doris than what Liz had given her during the entire conversation.

Liz and Joseph, appetites piqued by their morning crab pot expedition, attacked lunch with vigor.

Doris considered half of Joseph's Reuben sandwich would last her at least three days, but the young man dispatched all of it in a wink. She watched Joseph's expression when Liz spoke. Surprise. Not the sparkle of a smitten young man, but more the look a proud father might give his daughter. What to make of this? The implacable Doris would simply have to remain in the dark.

Joseph asked, "So, how goes the big mystery, Dad?"

"Think we might be onto something."

"Guess it'll take up your afternoon. Too bad. Liz and I are off on a hike. Thought maybe you could join us."

"We are? What about working on my tan?" Liz demanded.

"Shorts and a tank top, and we'll walk in the sun."

Michael asked, "Bivouacking?"

The two Marines exchanged a grin.

Liz demanded, "What's that?"

"You don't want to know. C'mon. Let's get a move on." Joseph already started to sound like a leader.

"Aye, aye, sir."

Liz stood in an exaggerated position of attention and rendered the reasonable facsimile of a salute.

When the *kids* were gone, Doris asked, "Bivouacking?"

"Camping out in a tent. Just a joke, Doris. You know how us guys are."

"Unfortunately."

"So what next? You said the chief stonewalled us. Maybe him?"

"Let's go see Leo first. We need a better read on the chief."

Michael felt he no longer had the lead role in their *case*.

Fifteen minutes later, Doris and Michael stood on the dock beside the *Rebound*.

Leo greeted them, "Twice in one day? A double treat." He called to his wife who went about chores below decks. "Bert! Get up here. Company."

Roberta climbed topside, her pleasure in spotting Michael signaled by placing a hand to her hair.

"Ahoy!" came the universal greeting among boaters.

Michael exclaimed, "Ahoy right back at you!"

Doris winced, not too excited about Roberta's enthusiastic greeting which seemed exclusively for Michael. She wanted to say 'I'm here too,' but didn't.

"Come aboard," Leo invited. "All coffeed out, or should we put on a pot? Sun's not quite over the yardarm, or I'd offer something stiffer."

"It is on the east coast," Roberta offered.

"We're fine," Michael replied.

The four sat comfortably in the deck chairs on *Rebound*'s fantail.

Leo broke the ice. "So, how's the day going? Guess this has to do with the investigation?"

Michael took a breath, but Doris cut him off. "We need to know more about the chief."

"Oh he—"

Leo interrupted his wife and through furrowed eyebrows asked, "What about him?"

"Doris thinks he knows more than he's telling."

"What did he say?"

Michael related the substance of their morning conversation.

"Wow! What do you figure was going on at the Hawke farm?"

Leo asked the question while Roberta looked on.

"Endless possibilities," Michael said. "Illegal farm workers seems a natural, but maybe its marijuana or other drugs, who knows?"

Leo offered, "Enough *other drugs* in a truck that size would represent a lotta scratch."

Michael said, "Yeah, but we need to consider all of the possibilities. I think this case extends beyond the possible murder of Thomas Hawke."

"You know, that never occurred to me. Why, I always focused on ... well, his son was pissed off ... excuse me, Doris."

Doris looked at Roberta for some sign of anger on her part for having been excluded from the apology, but saw none.

Leo continued, "I guess everyone believed Frederick was the prime suspect."

"But he wasn't here when it happened."

Placing a hand on Michael's arm, Doris said, "Let Leo explain. Why did you suspect him?"

He answered, "Motive. Frederick the playboy didn't like the idea of being cut off. Frankly, I think the story from the chief is a smokescreen."

Michael asked, "Why do you say that?"

"The farmers were unhappy about not being able to compete with Hawke. But that's no longer a problem now that Frederick's running the show. A happy ending out there, so I guess everybody wants to leave sleeping dogs lie."

Michael said, "But there's still the issue of Thomas's death. And from my read, Frederick was miles from the scene."

Seeing the conversation had made a complete circle, Doris asked, "Could it have been the chief?"

"No," said Michael. "He's not a killer. At least not in my book."

Leo said, "He was a submariner in World War II. Didn't those guys shoot survivors from the ships they sunk? He mighta done it ... killed old Thomas off. You know how devoted he is to his boss, Bushnell. A lot of motive there."

Doris turned to Michael. "Well?"

"The chief is a seaman. Necessities of war might make him leave a man struggling in the water. But murder him? I don't think so. I've been in combat, Leo. Nobody likes to kill a fellow human being. A few maybe, but about in proportion to the rest of society. The chief doesn't fit the pattern."

Leo remained silent.

"Look, Leo, Doris and I are headed back to talk with the chief. Thanks a lot for the help."

"You'll let me know what you find out?"

"Of course. You've been very helpful. We might need to lean on you for more. Okay?"

The chief looked up at them through squinted eyes, then down to his watch. "I thought you'd be back before this."

Doris took the lead. She wanted to milk this comment. "Why do you say that, Chief?"

"Been around long enough to read women like a book. I could tell you were not happy with my story."

"So what's the right one?"

Michael posed the question before Doris turned the *case* into a one woman show.

The chief looked directly at Doris and asked, "Why were you suspicious?"

"Because you've been through far too much to remain passive during the opportunity you had at the Hawke farm. You knew how much was at stake for Peter Bushnell and too loyal to sit on your thumbs with an opportunity like the one you had."

The chief looked at Michael. "Got your sights set on this woman? You could do a hell of a lot worse."

"Flattery will get you everywhere, Chief. Except with me. Now out with it."

Inwardly, Doris basked in her apparent success.

"Okay. Nothing to lose here. When I saw the truck back up, I sidled around to the back of the outbuilding. Someone left the rear door open, and I let myself in. First, all I heard were voices, loud, demanding, telling people what to do. The replies were timid and in a foreign language. Not Spanish. I heard enough of that from migrant workers in the area."

"Were they illegals?" Michael demanded.

"I believe so. Why else would Hawke be hiding them?"

"So you think that's why Hawke was able to operate at such low costs?"

"You damn betcha. He had them over a barrel. 'Work for me for peanuts or I'll turn you over to Immigration.' An offer they couldn't refuse."

"You see them? I mean actually? Not just heard them," said Doris.

"See 'em? Was so damn close, I could spit on 'em." They surprised me and turned down the hall I was hiding in, so I jumped into a broom closet. Then they stopped just outside and were talking away, when all of a sudden this young kid opens the closet."

Doris betrayed rare emotion. "My God, what did you do, Chief?"

"I held a finger to my mouth and patted my coat to make him think I had a gun in it. The poor kid was terrified. He grabbed a broom, slammed the door, and I heard him run away down the hall. Waited in there till it got quiet, for about five minutes, then slipped out the way I came in."

"So Peter knows about this? Anybody else?"

"Nobody. And I never said a word to Peter, either. He's my friend. If I told him, it might've put him in a position of having to do something he didn't want to do."

Doris and Michael exchanged glances that confirmed a mutual thought that Leo didn't tell all he knew either.

"Look, Chief, you gotta understand ... we're hearing so much we don't know who to believe."

"That's your problem."

Michael regarded the chief's logic a setback, but not Doris.

"No, Chief, it's your problem. You just said you witnessed importing of illegal immigrants and didn't advise the authorities. That makes you an accessory to the fact."

She winged it, and the chief saw through her like a pane of glass.

"I saw what appeared to be migrant workers. There's a lot of them in Eastern Washington. How did I know they were illegal?"

The three sat silent while the chief's words settled in.

He went on. "Look, Thomas Hawke's death was an accident. But speculation on it diverts attention from the real issue: illegals."

"So why are you so sure it was accidental?"

"Because I was there when he died."

Doris and Michael did a terrible job of masking their astonishment.

On the morning of Thomas Hawke's death, Stanley Porter lingered in a luxurious stretch then climbed from his bunk. Peter Bushnell slept soundly in the main bunkroom of the 27-foot Ranger sailboat.

The chief lit a propane burner and set a pot of the remains of last night's coffee on it. He'd rather have a *Fox Peter,* World War II Navy phonetic pronunciation of FP, or fresh pot. It would have to keep till he returned, for a crimson dawn already made its presence known in the northeastern sky above Roche Harbor. *Red sky in the morning, the sailors take warning,* he thought. He needed to get out to those pots before sunup. The chief knew he would be over limit and needed the cover of darkness.

The pot came to a boil and he doused the burner. He poured himself a cup then dumped it over the side, deciding he did not need coffee bad enough to have it chew up his insides like this would do. He poured it well outboard to protect the hull from being eaten away and felt sorry for any water creatures that might be in the area.

The chief climbed into Peter's Zodiac and the outboard caught after the third pull. *Better tune it.* He throttled the engine to not disturb nearby sleeping *boaties,* then made his way seaward toward the crab pot buoys.

Approaching the end of I dock, the chief noticed Thomas Hawke's *Vega* to be dark, save for the anchor lights. He'd not have noticed Thomas standing on the seaward side, but the magnate illuminated his face while lighting a cigar.

The chief wished a private audience with Thomas, but knew he sat too far down the totem pole for this to be in the cards. *What was it my old skipper used to call it? A target of opportunity? Why not?* The chief slowed and moored just forward of the *Vega,* and slipped aboard.

"Morning, Mr. Hawke."

Thomas turned, his look one of complete astonishment. "You? What the hell are you doing on my boat?"

"Heading out to tend the crab pots. Saw you alone up here and thought you'd like some company."

"Well you thought wrong. Now get the hell off here before I have you thrown off."

"Don't think you ought to do that Mr. Hawke. Least not till you hear me out. I know what's going on at that farm of yours."

Hawke bristled. "I told you, Porter. Get your ass off my boat!"

"Maybe I should talk to someone else then. Like Immigration, maybe?"

"Talk to whomever you want."

Thomas Hawke reached behind a freezer chest and picked up a baseball bat kept there for killing fish that had been reeled aboard and brandished it at the chief.

"Tell them about those illegals' barracks you operate in the outbuilding of your spread. You think they won't come out there with a warrant?"

"Do you know who you're talking to? What the hell is this? Blackmail? I wouldn't try that with me, you bastard."

"I'm not asking anything for me. Just take the pressure off my boss, Peter Bushnell, and I can forget everything I saw."

"Threaten me, you son of a bitch."

Thomas swung the bat at the chief's head who staved it off with his arm. Hawke swung again, this time so furious that he lost his balance. He stumbled backward a step then fell over the rail.

The chief heard a sickening thud concurrent with the splash as Hawke hit the water. He raced to the side and saw the form of Thomas Hawke lying still in the water. *What the hell have I got myself into now,* he thought.

The chief boarded the Zodiac and paddled to Hawke's motionless form that floated with face bobbing above and beneath the water surface in the gentle waves that lapped alongside the *Vega*. No bubbles emerged from the mouth and nose of Hawke's lifeless body.

His head had struck a huge log that floated nearby. The chief could do nothing.

Fortunately, no one saw him come or leave. He sped off into the night. *Best thing is to finish what I started out to do and play dumb when I get back.*

Doris and Michael sat quietly while the chief finished his story. "Why did you tell us this?"

"So you'd know there was no murder."

Michael asked, "Why should we believe you?"

"'Cause you know I'm telling the truth, Kincaid."

Michael sighed, unlike Harry Steele. "Yeah, I guess I do."

"No murder? I guess we're finished," said Doris.

"No!" the chief replied emphatically. "There's bigger stuff, but the accident on Hawke's boat ties my hands. I'd end up on the receiving end of a trumped up murder charge. You two have got to take it on."

Doris asked, "What bigger stuff?"

"Illegals," said the chief. "You got no idea what misery those people go through. I'm sure Frederick nipped it in the bud at the Hawke place, but somebody else has picked up on it, and you gotta find out who."

Chapter 9

An early afternoon sun looked down on Roche Harbor from a cloudless azure sky. Doris and Michael walked side by side with a casual grace. Neither betrayed evidence of indulgences by typical mid-fifties couples.

The hint of Michael's limp could still be detected, though a late summer tan all but obscured his souvenir scar from Vietnam. He had long ago decided to dress for comfort and to let the chips fall where they may. He'd chosen white shorts and tan T-shirt for this lovely day.

Doris's light brown hair bore sun highlights of summer. She wore shorts also, and though not having had as much sun as Michael, her legs reflected good care of herself. A vivid red tank top rounded off her outfit. More sensitive to appearances than Michael, Doris's mind sought perceptions of passersby and people seated on fantails of moored pleasure craft.

Thinking of Liz and Joseph, she thought, *Eat your hearts out, kids.* She said to Michael, "Didn't the chief's story blow your hat in the creek?"

Enthusiasm for the game had diminished since learning Porter's story. Did this make her an accessory?

Michael sensed her feelings. "I never passed myself off as the real thing, Doris."

She wished he'd select a pet name for her. *But what to expect from the retired marine-British literature combination?*

He continued, "But I had to learn a little if only in self-defense. Expect the unexpected. Don't be discouraged if a hot lead becomes a dead end. Most of them do, at least it's that way in my books. Everybody is a suspect until you nail the bad guy."

"Including the chief?"

Michael really didn't think so. There is a certain connection among military veterans. Though he considered Stanley Porter might have used this as a shield, Michael believed it unlikely.

"Everybody, till we finger the bad guy."

"He seems like such a sweetheart. The crusty exterior is like ore rock around gold," Doris offered. "Illegals? Isn't it common knowledge that much of the farm help in eastern Washington is there illegally?"

"If you're going to be a sleuth, Doris, you've got to hit those questions when the door opens. Should have asked the chief that when he mentioned it. I flat out didn't think of it."

"Next time?" she replied in an uncharacteristic timid voice.

"Next time." Michael went on, "Big problem is with no official status we can't get warrants to dig out information."

"Like?"

"Remember *Deep Throat* of Watergate fame? Follow the money. If something big goes on here, you know big bucks have to be involved. Ben and Ceely Shultz. Do they look like a couple able to afford fifty-eight feet of top quality yacht?"

"One or the other might've had rich parents."

"Possibly. But that's the sort of stuff we need to know. Maybe head over there and poke around." Michael suggested.

"Why not? It's a little early in the afternoon, but a glass of Chardonnay would sit pretty well about now."

An admiring glance from a passing young marina dockhand caused her to think, *See, I was right.*

They continued their walk to the extreme northwest finger of the boat docks, passing magnificent pleasure craft along the way. Occasionally, a light aircraft could be heard as it passed overhead and made its way into the western sky.

What a great country, he thought. This made Michael ponder the true meaning of his service. In the wake of how it had been so poorly perceived by many Americans, he often felt a need to reassure himself. *This is what America is all about. Opportunity for those with the mettle to act upon it. This is what I fought for. Screw everybody who doesn't see it that way.*

Liz and Joseph sat opposite each other at a roadside picnic table, munched on energy bars and satisfied thirsts with bottled waters. She had picked up on Marine Corps jargon quickly. "We gonna hike another twenty klicks, or go back now, Second Lieutenant Unger, sir?"

Joseph went along. "Suck it up, maggot! We're just getting started."

Their bodies glistened with a light sweat earned during what he termed their cross-country march. A soft breeze caressed them and evaporated skin moisture to create a refreshing coolness.

"You love this *Corps* stuff, don't you, Picky?"

Liz noted his deliberate and calculated responses. A challenge. She normally knew what strings to pull among her men friends to learn what she wanted. However, she found Joseph to be an enigma. According to information gleaned from her mother, Michael's intelligence exceeded the norm. Liz concluded this likely had been passed down to his son.

"The Marine Corps seems right for me. Infantry has the greatest appeal, but I'll know a lot better when I finish training at Pendleton."

"What else is there? I mean what choices?"

"Marine air, fighters or maybe helicopters."

"You mean flying around in jets? Like Tom Cruise in *Top Gun*? I don't see you doing that, and I sure don't see you singing *you lost that loving feeling*. Face it, Picky. You belong on a horse, with feathers in your hat, a sword and everything."

He smiled at her. *Listens a lot more than I thought.* Liz didn't miss a word of what he'd told her of the Civil War Gettysburg campaign.

"You mean I was born a hundred and fifty years too late?"

"Something like that. Seriously, Picky, aren't the marines about," she'd tread carefully with this one, "like violence and killing?"

The unexpected comment left Joseph determined not to say anything stupid. "I like to think of it as countering that. An old saying goes, 'The worst enemy or best friend you can have is a Marine.'"

He studied her face, but she revealed nothing. They sat a moment of unusual silence, each to give the other's mind a chance to assess the new direction from their normal flippant exchanges. A new thing for them: serious conversation.

Liz broke it. "How do your friends feel about you doing this? I know Michael is proud, but what about your adoptive parents?"

"Mom wrings her hands a bit, but Dad seems okay. Look, Liz. Bottom line is a man does what he believes he has to do."

They fell back into an awkward silence. Joseph sensed she wanted to say more, but revealed an uncharacteristic reluctance.

He continued with, "It's all about freedom. That includes free speech. Tell me what you think. I won't be offended."

"A good way to put it, if my brother Ralphie wanted to go in the service, I'd discourage him."

Joseph retorted almost before Liz had spoken. "Why would you do that?"

"You said you'd take no offense."

"Sorry," said Joseph. And then using a softer tone, "Why would you do that?"

"I'm not against the military. It's just I think there are too many better things to do. And if we went to war, I'd be worried sick."

Liz sensed her logic did not set well with Joseph and avoided his eyes.

"Why are other things better?"

His measured words did not completely remove the edge.

"Because he wouldn't be in any danger and not have to kill anybody."

"That is a downside of the profession, Liz. But the belief is the more prepared we are, the less likely that will happen."

She nodded but continued to avoid his eyes.

"There are other sides of the coin for all professions," he continued, "take sports media. A lot of people believe athletes are vastly overpaid, then expect the public to buy top of the line venues for them to play in."

"What's that got to do with the media end?"

"They lionize athletes and make it easier for the public to go along."

Joseph instantly regretted his remark. He had sharpened a weak stick simply to strike back at her allegation over the Corps.

This time she caught his eye. "Maybe we better get going on this hike thing."

They walked in silence for a time. Joseph reflected on their circumstance. He had developed an attraction for Liz, and suspected he had just written off his chances. Admitting one is wrong is about as tough as it gets for a twenty-five year old male.

"I apologize for saying what I did, Liz. That was a cheap shot."

Liz's face remained expressionless and she made that clear by looking directly at him. "It's not a big deal, Joseph."

Oh crap, he thought. *What the hell happened to Picky?*

She continued, "It's a long weekend at Roche, nothing more. Come tomorrow, we're both long gone. No need to get upset about anything."

"Hello!" called Ben Schultz from atop a ladder leading to the afterdeck of *Yakima Gold*. "'Bout time you two showed up here. Come aboard. Sun's close enough to the yardarm."

Michael waved. "Thank you, Ben. Be right up."

Several white puffs of cirrus clouds marred the otherwise clear sky. A light northwest breeze sent ripples plinking against pristine white sides of the boat's carbon fiber hull. A ladder of mahogany steps, capped with non-slip treads led to the fantail, where Ben and Ceely Schulz greeted them.

Ceely called out, "Good to see you guys."

"You too," Doris replied as all exchanged handshakes.

"Yep, sun's near the yardarm." Ben raised a hand to shield his eyes while he confirmed his assessment. "What's your pleasure on this hot and thirsty afternoon? A brewski for me and an ABC for Ceely."

Doris knew Ben fished her in but bit anyway. "ABC?"

Ceely replied, "Anything but Chardonnay. Ben simply lives to use that term."

"Hope that doesn't mean there's none aboard. Doris's been salivating for one over the last hour." Michael had stuck his chin out a mile.

Doris came back without hesitation. "Looks like we have similar tastes in men, Ceely. Clowns."

"You got that right. Just for that, you two go get the drinks while we ladies lounge."

The men did not have far to go. The cabin inside the fantail featured a dining area and wet bar. They shortly returned with the libations, Doris's Chardonnay, a Pinot Grigio for Ceely and beer for the guys.

Ben declared, "Welcome aboard and to a great weekend at Roche." After they raised glasses and toasted, Ben continued. "So, what've you guys been up to?"

"Enjoying the weather, eating, walking about the docks, eating, catching the sunset, eating. Think you get the picture. You met Joseph and Liz on the *Vega*. Bottomless pits and we can't let them faint from hunger. Unfortunately, watching them primes the pump. Diet after I get home."

"Give me a break," Ben complained. "You two could eat a cow between you, and it wouldn't show." He shifted gears abruptly. "So have you done any sleuthing, detective Steele?"

"Matter of fact, yes. Someone slipped aboard *Vietvet* Friday night. Took some doing, but we determined it was a sea lion."

"C'mon, Michael. You know what I mean ... the Hawke mystery."

Ceely reacted with an interested look but said nothing.

Michael replied, "To be honest, we have. Turns out to be quite an exercise. Might have uncovered enough material for a new Harry Steele thriller."

Doris successfully masked her astonishment. *He's good,* she thought. *What a cover. Maybe he really should consider becoming the real thing.*

"Well how's it shaping up? Will Ceely and I be in it?"

"Always change names to protect the guilty. Promise not to let it out, but your characters turn out to be the heavies."

"Put me down for two copies. One for us, and the other for our attorney."

The four shared a good laugh.

Ben continued, "So we are the murderers?"

"Do you want to be? Just like the police reported: there was no murder, but certain people use it to divert attention from another and more profitable venue."

"Like what?"

Ceely replied too quickly. This got her a frown from Ben.

Michael expected and caught it. "Can't give away the whole book, now, can I?"

"Oh come, now, Michael. You gotta throw us at least a bone," Ben replied.

"Illegals," but this time Michael's gaze fastened on Ceely. She gave the anxious look he figured she'd give her husband.

"We must let Michael off the hook, Ceely. He's on holiday and deserves a break. Have you watched the colors ceremony? You're an ex-Marine. What do you think?"

An ex-Marine? What in hell is that? Once a Marine, always a Marine. Michael could not understand why the rest of the world did not know this. He took it personal as it brought to mind the lousy welcome he got from fellow Americans on his return from Vietnam.

Doris sensed Michael's feeling and said, "Michael stood tall, straight and silent. I was proud to stand beside my Marine."

Doris gave Michael a look that dissolved his irritation.

Conversation lightened while the four finished their drinks. Doris and Michael politely turned down Ben's offer of a second round.

"Long night ahead," Michael reasoned. "Trying to avoid having the Dean write my liver a letter of commendation."

Blank looks from the Schultzes caused Doris to explain, "It's a service thing."

Good-byes spoken, Doris put her arm in Michael's. They chorused a thank you and left.

Doris and Michael well out of earshot, Leo Walters emerged from below decks. "Do they know anything?"

Ben related the substance of their conversation.

Leo replied, "Nothing to worry about from a half-assed wannabe detective. Do you know if they got Hawke off the *Vega* so we can use it tonight?"

The docks filled quickly with happy people walking to and fro, readying themselves for what promised to be a spectacular evening. A lighthearted aura deepened as the bright midday sun yielded to golden yellow.

Doris and Michael had seconds at the Madrona Bar and Grill overlooking the harbor.

She asked, "Did Ceely look uncomfortable?"

"Clearly they know something they're not sharing," Michael replied.

"You think something bad's going on? Should we be telling the police about this?"

Michael sipped at his Heineken. "What do we have to tell? We discussed a new murder mystery and the woman listening looked uncomfortable?"

Doris nodded her agreement. "Then what do you think we should do?"

"Not a lot," he replied. "Maybe poke around a bit more and when we get back, I'll bounce what I know off Jim Epsom. With all his years at Clallam County Sheriff, he'll know what to make of it. And he has access to a lot of stuff we don't."

She liked his use of the pronoun, we. Women see far more in such subtleties than guys do.

"Sounds good to me. Not a lot of risk in that, I guess." He took a breath to say *Underestimating risk is what gets most people into trouble,* but didn't. Michael changed the subject. "Wonder what the kids are up to?"

"Likely they're hiking through the old lime quarries, getting first class panoramic views of the outer islands and Canadian Gulf Islands. Breathtaking."

Michael smiled. "Depends on who's in charge. History buff Joseph would much prefer the McMillin's historical mausoleum. Understand it was built as a memorial to John S. McMillin's family and for those things in which he believed. He incorporated symbols from Masonry, the Bible, Sigma Chi fraternity and his own views of family unity."

"And you say Joseph's the history buff."

"Been here a few times with Ada and Jim Epsom and did some poking around. You know Theodore Roosevelt stayed here, and his signature is in the guest register?"

"I do now." Her smile dissolved his serious expression. She had other and more important things on her mind. "Hope they remembered to take something along to eat and drink."

"You can take that to the bank," Michael replied.

"How far did they plan to hike? Not all the way to the British Camp, I hope."

"If Joseph has his way, they will."

"And Liz is hardheaded enough to not say uncle. They'll be beat out for the rest of the day."

"Wanna bet they'll close the bar tonight?"

Doris shook her head. "George Bernard Shaw was right. Youth is wasted on the young."

"And I'm supposed to be the Brit Lit Prof. Sorry, you haven't seen very much of Joseph, but that came into the cards when Liz entered the mix. How do you think they get along?"

"Good, I think. They seem to enjoy each other. It would have been cruel to make him hang out with the old folks. But knowing Joseph, he'd have soldiered on. Wonder who he gets that from?"

"Touché," he admitted. "Look! Isn't that Peter Bushnell heading this way?"

"Perfect," Doris replied. "Invite him over. Maybe he can clear up the chief's illegals remark."

Michael intercepted Peter and asked him to join them.

"Never could say no to a pretty face, Michael. Not yours, of course. Hi, Doris. Word around the harbor is Michael's the luckiest guy up here."

"Flattery works every time, Peter. You and the chief enjoying your stay?"

"The chief enjoys everything he does," Peter replied. "A great sailing partner. But he wants to sail us to Hawaii and in a twenty-seven foot sailboat. He wants to navigate with a sextant."

Doris said, "Well don't sign me up for the trip."

Michael added, "Me neither. How often do you get to do this kind of trip?"

"Not often enough. The chief is totally retired, so anytime is a good one for him. Now me … still have to put bread on the table."

"Curse of the working class," Michael added. "Know the feeling."

Peter asked, "Aren't your summers free? I mean when school is out?"

"A myth with a purpose. Best reason known to abate pay raises. Next comes summer school, which strangely enough requires teachers."

Doris weighed in, "And during academic year, a Prof puts in at least one hour for every two he spends in class. Lesson plans, grading papers, individual student meetings. Cost of education is a bargain, believe me."

"But no complaints," said Michael. "It doesn't really seem like work when you enjoy what you do. Teaching is very satisfying."

"Same thing the chief says about the Navy. Couldn't believe they paid him for having so much fun. And they still do. Navy retirement."

Michael held a totally different view he didn't share. *How much is enough to pay a man to dodge bullets?* But his own retirement pay, coupled with his salary at the college, left him fairly comfortable.

He liked the idea of opening small talk. They should not make Peter suspicious of anything by jumping in too quickly so they dallied among a number of topics such as people watching, cuteness of passing dogs on leashes, quality of some of the more spectacular boats in the harbor and skilled ship handling exhibitions or lack thereof.

Doris broke the ice. "We talked to the chief earlier today, Peter. He said something I didn't quite understand. He expressed concerns over the way illegals are treated in eastern Washington. Can you shed any light?"

Peter's soft look folded into a curious one. "That's unusual. Can't believe he knows anything I don't know. Wouldn't say accommodations are exactly top of the line, but the migrant workers seem quite happy. Suspect what they have south of the border is not much better, if at all."

Michael added, "The term, illegals, surprised me. To my knowledge, much of the migrant farm help falls into that category. But Immigration turns a blind eye, because help is needed at harvest time."

Peter said, "That pretty much tracks with what I know."

Doris noted. "I read recently that undocumented farm workers in Vermont are held prisoner, too frightened to leave the confines of private property for fear they'll be picked up by police and deported."

"I've never heard anything like that in eastern Washington. Just go downtown any evening during harvest in the tri-cities area and you need to speak Spanish if you want to get around. Look. If you're interested, I'll talk to the chief about it."

Michael replied, "No need to do that, Peter. The remark just struck me as odd."

"The old detective mind at work?"

"Hardly. Harry Steele is pure fiction, but I believe sometimes even my subconscious gathers material for the next book," Michael replied.

"A new one? When? Put me down for a copy."

Michael smiled. "Thanks. Can never have too many readers. Nothing definite yet. This is such a great place to set a mystery. I'm already thinking of an angle."

Peter offered to buy a round, but they fended him off. They needed no thirds, for a full evening remained ahead.

Chapter 10

Joseph stretched out on a mat to work on his tan but got up to greet Doris and Michael when they arrived back at the *Vietvet*.

Michael asked, "You leave Liz at the British Camp? Do I have to borrow Hawke's car and go get her?"

Joseph awakened from a half sleep. "Uh, no. She's below. Getting some shuteye, I think."

Uh-oh, Doris thought, *Liz missing out on all these rays and an opportunity to show guys her red bikini? Must be trouble in paradise.* "Maybe I'll run down and give sleeping beauty a nudge."

Joseph exclaimed, "Wow! It's after five. Shower time. While you're down there, Mrs. B., would you please toss up my toilet kit and a towel? I don't want to barge in on Liz if she's not decent."

"Sure, Joseph."

Turning to Michael, he asked, "Got some quarters, Dad?"

He needed them to operate the public showers at the head of the dock.

"Jim Epsom keeps a quarter jar in the locker above the sink. Run down and grab a handful when Doris says the coast is clear." Jim Epsom frequented Roche enough to be fully prepared. He sorted out his change and saved quarters for the *Vietvet* jar. "So … you guys have fun today?"

Joseph hesitated. "Well, yeah. Kinda. We just walked."

Michael had only limited time with his son, but enough with students his age to read body language. "Anything wrong?"

"Wrong? Why is anything wrong, Dad? I mean I'm just passing through here for a coupla days."

Michael asked quietly, "Liz irritated with you?"

He knew his son could talk the ears off a sleeping elephant. Perhaps Joseph had fire-hosed Liz with more historical data than the poor girl could absorb.

"Nothin's developing between us, if that's what you're getting at." Joseph was not good at blasé. "Look, Dad, a day or so, and I'll be up to my buns at Pendleton. Don't know when there'll be time for anything else."

Undeterred, Michael asked, "She say something to you?"

Joseph frowned. "She doesn't think much of the Corps."

"That what she said?"

"Not exactly. But it's clear that's how she feels."

"Look, son. Not many people see Marines like you and I do. If we let that stand in the way of friendships, we'd end up awful lonely. Jim Epsom and his wife, Ada, nearly split over the Vietnam War. While he was in country, slugging it out with the 'cong, Ada was back here demonstrating against the war. What a tragedy if they had let that stand in the way of what they've become."

"It's not like that, Dad. Liz and I are just two different people. She has her ways and I have mine."

Doris appeared and the conversation ended. "Toilet kit and towel, Joseph. And I brought the jar of quarters 'cause I didn't know how many you need."

"Thanks, Mrs. B."

Joseph readied himself for a walk up the dock and left.

Doris looked at Michael. "Well?"

"Well, what?"

"Are all people who write novels as easy to read as you are?"

He smiled. *What would life be like beside a woman with that much intuition?* He related the substance of his conversation with Joseph. "What's with Liz?"

"What she says or what I think?"

"I'm not stupid enough to choose anything but what you think," he replied.

"In a word, Liz has trouble with guys who don't bend around to her way of thinking."

"Well that's sure Joseph," Michael replied.

The somewhat peeved voice of Liz, emerged from below ready for her trip to the showers.

"What's sure Joseph?"

Michael took a breath to speak, but Doris interrupted. "He's his own man, honey. A rare bird this day and age."

Liz looked like she wanted to say more, but perhaps not in the presence of Michael. She walked off along the dock with her determined, athletic stride.

"She's a beauty," said Michael. "Notice all the heads she turns?"

"That's her problem. Too many of them, and she knows it. Maybe she believes that entitles her to a social leg up. Gets pretty irritated with guys she can't boss around."

Daughter like mother, only difference, Doris's approach is more mature.

It could have been a sore spot with him, but over the years, he learned to listen. By far, most of her things made sense, and he did not feel that going along in any way diminished his manhood. A smart man, he chose not to share this view with Doris.

"Well, let's hope they enjoy what's left of the weekend."

"They'll have fun," Doris said. "That's their jobs. Though she won't admit it, Liz considers Joseph a *hunk*, and likes to be seen with him." She paused then continued, "I think Liz is a little worried about our so-called case. Said she doesn't want us getting into anything scary."

"Did you tell about our plan to drop it on Jim Epsom?"

Doris liked the word *our* and that Michael infrequently used the personal pronoun *I*.

She smiled at him. "Not quite. Liz is young enough to get turned on by the thought of adventure. Just said it's nothing the two of us can't handle."

"Her response?"

"You know her, by now. Liz said, 'Whatever the hell that is.'" They shared a laugh.

Michael said, "What a fabulous evening."

The beautiful people began making their way up the docks for various cocktail and dinner venues offered by the resort, their fine clothing consistent with qualities of the crafts which bore them to Roche. Something about *boaties* makes them happier when they're around other *boaties*.

She asked, "Shower time?"

"We could save quarters and take one together?"

"Would Dean Benson approve?"

Michael looked about him. "He's nowhere in sight."

Doris shook her head. "Promises, promises. Now get your stuff and let's go."

The first stars made their appearance over Lime Kiln dock as the four sat down for a farewell dinner at the McMillin Restaurant. Doris had it right, no surprise. The edges on Liz's and Joseph's demeanors had diminished. Dancing had already started at the Madrona Bar and Grill downstairs from the McMillin and both looked forward to it.

The women wore the dressiest of the dresses they brought, while the men slipped by in slacks and sports shirts. Joseph, clearly pleased with the way Liz looked, stole what he mistakenly believed to be unnoticed glances at her.

Doris didn't miss a trick, but thought, *I wonder when Michael's going to look at me that way? Maybe if I dress up as Mary Queen of Scots, or Rowena in Ivanhoe. Something the old Brit Lit Prof can relate to.*

Joseph put away his second prime rib of the weekend without a sign of shame, while Michael looked on with envy. He and the ladies tested seafood entrees. Michael and Doris forewent desserts and had coffees.

Not the kids. Burnt crème for Liz and fresh cherry pie a la mode for Joseph. Once finished, they undertook transparent efforts to mask their desire to get downstairs to the dancing.

Neither flinched when Doris suggested that she and Michael needed to talk, and they disappeared like shots from a cannon.

After they left, Michael asked, "Talk about what?"

"About why we shouldn't make the kids sit here when they'd rather be downstairs."

"Your intuition is uncanny."

"About intuitive as noticing a tree just fell on you? How could you not see what drives them? You think maybe we could have a dance later?"

"Why not," he replied. "When I see what they do down there, my gimpy leg will fit right in. We'll be trend-setters, because I doubt anyone can duplicate it."

"The Viet hobble. Before we leave, it'll be the rage of the Harbor."

"Yeah, but I liked it better when dancing was a body contact sport. Look out on that dance floor. You can't tell who's dancing with whom."

"Trust a lit Prof to say it right."

"Right?"

"Who else uses the word *whom* in conversation?"

"I'm that bad?"

"You're that good, sweetie," she responded affectionately. *At Roche, everybody likes everybody a little better.*

They finished coffees and headed downstairs toward the music.

In the lounge, Michael pointed out a familiar form seated beside a Remy Martin at the bar. It was the chief.

"Let's sidle up to him, Doris. I'm sure an old Navy man will give up his seat to a lady."

"Depends," she replied, "on how many Remys he's put away. Not sure he'll be able to stand up."

She was right. The chief looked a bit looped. He made the offer of his stool, but Doris refused him. He gathered up his snifter and turned to face them.

Not to miss a sale, the bartender quickly approached the newcomers. Michael looked to Doris, who *let it all hang out* and ordered a lemon drop, declaring it was Roche and the calories be damned.

Pointing at the chief's snifter, Michael said, "I'll have one of those. Tell us, Chief. Where did a crusty old submariner acquire a taste for the good stuff?"

The chief related a World War II story wherein submariners, returning from patrols in the western Pacific, turned their ships over to a refit crew and spent their time ashore at the Royal Hawaiian Hotel in Honolulu at government expense. In the opening days of the war, their chances of not making it back, one in four, represented the highest casualty rate of any service, hence this special concession.

"Most of the guys drank beer," the chief explained, "but this sailor from New York, who ducked out of Yale in June of nineteen forty-one to join the Navy, ended up on my submarine. This infuriated his family 'cause he didn't join them at their mansion in Newport, Rhode Island that summer. Their loss, but we gained a helluva good torpedoman. Once, when we were at the Royal Hawaiian bar, he pointed to this funny looking bottle on the shelf and said his father drinks it all the time. Figured right away it must be good enough for me, then. The rest is history."

"You guys really earned it, Chief. The Royal Hawaiian was not good enough for you."

"Yeah." The chief did not want to talk about it and quickly changed subjects. "You know, there's only three true Cognacs: Remy, Martell, and Hennessey."

Eager to join the conversation, Doris asked, "What about Courvoisier, the Cognac of Napoleon?" She had questions for the chief that would have to keep.

"Not the real stuff. Gotta be from the Cognac region of France to qualify. Only those three come from there," the chief said with certainty.

Michael doubted but insufficiently certain, opted not to challenge this. He thought, *A true diamond in the rough.* He wondered how many brilliant people from America's first three decades of the twentieth century never came to fruition because of inability to afford college.

The barkeep arrived with their drinks.

Michael raised his glass. "To submariners! Thank you for your service, Chief."

They clinked glasses and drank.

The chief said, "Hear you picked up that gimp in Nam. You guys didn't do too bad either."

"I got a better toast," offered Doris. "Here's to having no one else to fight."

Again they raised their glasses. "Hear, hear," chorused the two veterans.

Michael wished he could share Doris's optimism. History is measured by wars fought for a variety of reasons, most inconsequential in terms of meaningful change, but never in the number of souls sacrificed.

Finally Doris asked the question she'd failed to ask earlier in the day. "Chief, this afternoon you mentioned *illegals* in eastern Washington. We're not sure what you meant."

The chief then related the story they heard the previous day, of Peter Bushnell's, Leo Walters', and the chief's winter visit to Thomas Hawke's farm. "Couldn't see exactly, but I'm sure there were people getting out of that truck … clearly a hush-hush operation."

"There're a lot of illegal Hispanics in eastern Washington."

"Who said anything about Hispanics?"

Both gave him questioning glances.

"Look. I already had too many Remys. Not a good time to talk, okay? Now why'n hell don't you ask this lady for a dance before this old submariner beats you to it?"

"If they played real music. C'mon, Chief. Look at the action out there." Michael pointed toward the dance floor. "Native American war dances weren't as wild as this."

The chief grinned. "Don't let the kids have everything. There's gotta be somethin' slow in the disc jockey's pile. Look at those old farts sittin' on their thumbs. The gold that runs

Roche comes outta their pockets and all they do is sit and watch. Get the DJ to play somethin' slow and they'll jump to their feet like it was the Star Spangled Banner."

Michael approached the DJ. He had to dig deep, but found a copy of Barbra Streisand's *The Way We Were*. Chief Porter hit the nail squarely on its head. At the first notes, *old farts* sprung to attention like a company of Marines if the commander in chief had just walked in. Sounds of popping joints filled the room. The kids, not knowing what to do, vacated the floor.

Michael stood before Doris. "Ma'am, the Sergeant Major requests the honor."

"That so, Sergeant Major?"

She took his hand and led him to the dance floor. There, they folded into each other's arms and swayed gently to the music.

Michael had not held her before then. There had been pecks good night, but always at a safe distance. He enjoyed the scent of her—a sensation that evaded him for many years, one he had come to believe was long over. He wondered if his body remained firm enough to impress her with no notion nothing could be further from her mind.

Joseph and Liz watched from the sidelines as Liz whispered, "Looks like a full-fledged preflight operation to me."

Doris and Michael walked hand in hand along the docks toward the *Vietvet*'s slip. Michael found himself wishing *the kids* had not come along and thought, *There's simply magic in this place.*

They reached the slip and climbed aboard. "Know we've already had a few, but how about a Chardonnay for the road?"

She sensed his frustration and the impossible situation of the *kids* showing up at any moment. Another drink would take the edge off for him.

"You'll never guess what I found poking around in the bunkroom. Would you believe Jim has a bottle of Hennessey down there? Not Remy, but—"

"That scoundrel! Never said a word about that to me, his true buddy."

Michael had polished off another Remy before leaving the lounge, and it showed.

"One more can't hurt," she rationalized and went below. She emerged with the bottle and a glass. "Not a snifter," she explained.

"Well, one simply has to make do, doesn't one?"

"I can take it back if this is not okay."

"Do that and I'll break the most beautiful arm it has ever been my pleasure to have been wrapped around me."

Michael waxed eloquent. She knew he didn't need another drink but poured it anyway.

Later, as they swayed on *Vietvet's* deck to sounds emanating from Doris's Sinatra collection, Peter Bushnell called from the dock. "Michael? Don't mean to interrupt, but do you have a moment?"

Never in Michael's life had he fewer moments to spare than right now, but ascension to full professor had left him too dignified to simply say no, or come back later. "Certainly, Peter, come aboard."

Doris asked, "Have a drink, Peter?"

"Yeah," said Michael, "but only if you can force down some twenty-five-year-old Cognac."

Peter quipped, "Contaminated by the chief, I see."

"Contaminated? I would choose a different term."

Doris poured him a stiff jolt. "Is this *guy* talk or can I stick around?"

"Doris, what man in his right mind would exclude you from the conversation?"

"Flattery works, Peter. We talked about that earlier today at the Madrona, but it's still true," she replied.

"Can't think of anything more. We toasted just about everything today, so here's mud in your eye, Peter."

"And yours," Peter replied. "You had a chat with the chief. Was he able to clear anything up for you?"

"Not a lot, actually. We discussed what he meant by *illegals* and he pleaded too many drinks."

"Oh," said Peter. "I guess he decided to open up to me when he got back to the boat. Look, Michael, I don't mean to barge in on your last night in Roche, but could you come by and talk with us? The chief could be onto, well, something significant."

"Sure you want to discuss this with me? I'm a hack, a mystery writer, not the real thing."

"But a lot's rubbed off in the process. What do you say?"

"Need my fellow sleuth?"

"I should be here for the kids," Doris interjected. "If they get back and find us gone, it might worry them. You go ahead, Michael. If it's anything we need to talk about, it should keep till you get back."

"Okay." *Even after all this, still no pet name.* Then Michael continued, "See you in a bit."

As the two walked off, Doris reflected upon the weekend with Michael and sensed they converged on permanency. He exhibited many qualities she admired, but knew there was more to it.

All their courtship experience had been gained as twenty-year-olds, now easily recognizable when one or the other made a move. This resulted in abrupt laughter interrupting would-be intimate moments.

Single couples, with no children, or previous baggage of a failed marriage, could enter relationships far less encumbered. Doris felt no need for a new husband before Michael came into her life, hence nothing to ponder. All that changed now and even though her children reached adulthood, they did matter. Liz, a free spirit, would be fine with the devil if that's who her mom chose.

Ralph, a mirror image of his sister, looks the same, but everything else reversed. It took a long time for him to be okay with his dad's new wife. Ralph would likely be defensive on seeing his mom with another man, as though he had to protect her. Yes, Ralphie would take some handling. Maybe Liz could help.

Doris enjoyed a quiet laugh at the thought. *Who in their right mind would invite Liz the compulsive rationalizer into this?*

The chief's snoring could be heard a full twenty yards from the *Sunskip*. He slept soundly on the upper deck portside transom.

Michael asked, "You sure the chief is up for this? He sounds occupied to me."

Michael himself continued to perceive things through the slight haze of his additional Cognac.

"The chief snaps to pretty quickly," said Peter. "Like an old warhorse to the sound of cannon fire." He shook the chief gently and Peter's prophecy was fulfilled. The elderly submariner was immediately awake and coherent.

"Michael Kincaid's here, Chief. We need to talk about what you saw at the Hawke farm a few winters back."

The chief rubbed his eyes. "Where do you want to start? You both know everything I saw."

"Your gut, Chief," said Peter. "Like the time you got us through Deception Pass in a heavy fog, all on hunches."

Stanley Porter looked back and forth between Michael and Peter to buy time. He preferred not to blurt out opinions without thinking them through completely. He described the truck unloading incident.

"It had to be something pretty big for all that security to be in place. Four of the meanest hombres you ever saw, just standing there to be sure whatever they were doing was not observed. The head guy was clearly pissed when he spotted me outside, having a smoke."

Michael asked, "Why do you think it was people? Illegals, you called them."

"A hunch. The truck was big. Anything other than human beings walking off would take longer to unload."

Michael said, "Not likely immigrant farm workers, because everyone knows that's no big deal. Right?"

"I'd say so," the chief agreed.

Peter asked, "You think it was people and not immigrant farm workers? What the hell could it be?"

"Something damn important with all that security in place. As much as I ever saw in the Navy."

"Listen," Peter said, "I think we should discuss this with Frederick Hawke. I know he wasn't there at the time, but it's his farm, and he might be able to shed some light."

"Wait," Michael said then asked, "What if he's involved? We might be sticking our head in a noose. Maybe it's time to let the police take over."

"No. Frederick's a straight arrow," Peter replied. "That I know for sure. He's likely cleaning up some mess left by his father. Thomas Hawke was a son of a bitch. Nothing he'd do would surprise me. Besides, what could happen to us up here? Too many boats and people around."

"Like on the night of Thomas's death?"

"That was different. An accident. Even the police said so. C'mon. Let's head over to the *Vega* and put this thing to bed."

When they reached the *Vega*, Michael excused himself and walked across the dock to tell Doris what was happening. The *kids* had still not showed.

"Like I told you," Michael said, "those poor tired darlings will close the bar tonight. See you in a bit."

Doris sat below decks, a copy of Michael's first novel had fallen from her lap, her head cocked to one side in sleep and the reading glasses slipped to the end of her nose.

Liz awakened her, "Hi, Mom. Gotcha! Saw that preflight work on the dance floor. Where's Michael? Betcha he's still in your bed."

Fully awake, Doris said, "Not a chance, smarty-pants, Michael's off the boat. He, Peter Bushnell and the chief are aboard the *Vega* visiting Mr. Hawke."

The remark startled Joseph. "That can't be!   Remember, Liz? Mr. Hawke left the island this afternoon for a couple days of business. He drove by when we were walking and offered us a lift.   Peter Bushnell knows this because he was driving the car."

Doris exclaimed, "Oh, my God!"

"That's not the worst part. When we came down the dock, the *Vega* was heading down the channel, outward bound."

Chapter 11

Peter showed Michael and the chief to Frederick Hawke's study aboard the *Vega*. "I'll go get him," Peter said.

Michael grit his teeth. *Damn,* he thought. *What a helluva time to be snockered.* He at least knew his mind would not be at its best. But could he muster the discipline to avoid saying or doing anything stupid? The chief drank much more but seemed in better control.

Peter astounded them when he returned, not with Frederick, but Miguel Vargas.

Miguel plopped himself into Frederick's chair. He looked at the two men seated before him then to Peter Bushnell. "So, what's this about?"

Only a trace of his usual heavy Hispanic accent remained.

"I think these two know too much."

The chief and Michael exchanged astonished glances.

Michael demanded, "What's this?"

Miguel answered, "You have a saying in this country. Curiosity killed the cat. Maybe this is a prophecy about to be fulfilled." All traces of the loyal and obedient servant had disappeared. "What do they know, Peter?"

"About the people stashed at the old Hawke farm."

"And how do they know that?"

"Porter, here. Coupla years ago, he witnessed a load being dumped at the farm."

The expression of pain on the chief's face transcended lines etched by many years at sea. His dearest friend, the man with whom he had willingly and happily shared most of his declining years, his trusted sailing partner had just betrayed him.

Vargas's face folded into a frown. "You never said anything about this before. Why not?"

Peter replied, "I only learned of it today. Likely, because super sleuth got involved."

Miguel replied, "So my plan backfired. Mr. Kincaid, you were only supposed to get the case on Frederick reopened. Now look what you've gone and done."

Sharp enough to know they were in serious trouble, Michael chose his words carefully, though still under the effects of too much alcohol. *This should be harmless enough,* "I don't know what you're talking about. I'm just up here at Roche, enjoying a beautiful weekend. If it's okay with you, the chief and I will leave and forget all about whatever you and Bushnell are talking about."

At that instant, he felt the *Vega* shudder as her propellers pulled her in reverse out into the harbor.

Vargas said in a soft voice, "A bit late for that, Kincaid. Why don't you come along with us and satisfy your curiosity? You've poked hard enough to see what is happening here, and so you shall. Peter, show these two to their cabin, please."

The chief and Michael turned to face Peter Bushnell confronting them with a pistol in his hand. His impassive face showed no trace of remorse over betraying the chief. Peter conducted them to a well-appointed guest cabin, closed the door behind them and locked it.

The chief looked sternly at Michael. "Any ideas?"

Michael wondered what Harry Steele would do but came up blank.

When Peter Bushnell returned to the study, Miguel Vargas had been joined by Leo Walters and Ben Schulz.

Peter asked, "Well, what do we do with those two?"

Miguel replied, "Fortunately, both have been drinking. Tomorrow morning, two drowned bodies will be found near the harbor, not far from the capsized Zodiac from *Vega*. I will report the Zodiac as missing. Blood alcohol contents of the corpses will explain the rest."

Doris, Liz and Joseph absorbed the shocking facts that had just been revealed.

Liz demanded, "Call the police. Now!"

Doris asked, "What would we tell them? Michael disappeared about an hour ago, and we think he's on the *Vega*."

Joseph agreed. "We don't have enough to get anyone to spring into the action. Let's think this through. Exactly what happened, Mrs. Baker?"

Relating the events of the evening, Doris explained what she and Michael uncovered.

Joseph asked, "Are you sure the chief was with them? Maybe we should go to Bushnell's sailboat to see if he's there?"

Her growing concern obvious, Doris replied, "No, he was with them. I saw him go aboard."

"It'll be okay, Mom," Liz put a hand on her mother's shoulder. "Joseph will think of something. Won't you, Picky?"

Mmm, Picky again ... at least for the moment, he thought.

"Look, Mrs. Baker. Let me have your cell phone. Before the *Vega* gets out of sight, I'll borrow Leo Walters' dinghy and follow them out. Maybe I'll pick up something suspicious enough to call the Coast Guard."

Liz exclaimed, "I'll go with you!"

"No, wait," Doris ordered. "You'll need to talk to me and you have my phone."

"Use Dad's. Isn't that it on top of the fridge?"

"Yes," Doris replied, "I've used it before and know how."

"Let's get going, Picky, before we lose sight of the *Vega*."

"No, Liz. If something goes wrong, we don't need two people getting caught up in it. I'll go alone."

"Okay, macho man, you think a woman would be useless? Screw you. Who died and left you the boss?"

Joseph's voice remained calm and steady, "I never said anything like that. Simple axiom. 'Never expose any more troops than those needed for the mission.'"

"Don't try that crap on me, Picky. I'm not a Marine."

"You're right, Liz. If you were, you'd go out, and I'd stay here."

Damn, he thought. *Said two dumb things in the same day.*

A furious Liz snapped, "You don't tell me what to do!"

Doris saw valuable time wasted with useless bickering and intervened. "Joseph's right," she said. "We don't need two in that little boat. The wind's picked up. Joseph, are you sure this is safe?"

"There's no other choice. We need something to hang our hat on before we can call in the authorities. All we have now is an *It'll keep till morning set of circumstances.* If it's what we think, morning could be too late."

He looked at Liz, hoping for redemption, but found none then recorded his dad's cell phone number and left the *Vietvet*.

The chief asked, "What do we do now?"

He knew the situation was grim, but both had been in dire straits before and they knew only cool heads would free them.

"Nothing till we think it through," Michael replied. "How you doing? Musta been a real kick in the ass … Peter turning on you."

The chief's face remained impassive. "That later. Right now, we gotta figure a way out of here. You any good at picking locks, detective?"

Michael replied, "No. From the sound of it, it was a deadbolt. We gotta figure this room is no accident. There's no latch or knob on the inside. Any ideas on what these turkeys are up to, Chief?"

"Somethin' bad enough to risk kidnapping. That's a big time offense last I heard, and that's what's happening to us. Damn, how'd I let myself be led down the primrose."

"You trusted the wrong guy. All of us do that once in a while." Michael thought of his first wife, but quickly dismissed the notion. After all, she brought Joseph into the world. "It's likely Thomas Hawke was involved. It's now clear why you were tossed out of the meeting when Bushnell, Walters and you went to the Hawke farm."

"That means Leo and Ben are involved too," said the chief then he asked, "What about Frederick?"

"Doubtful, but he might have been getting close. That's why Vargas wanted the investigation reopened. Give Frederick something else to think about. Talk about being foolish, Chief. Look at the way I got fished in."

"Yeah," the chief replied. "But right now, we got other problems. The way I see it, somebody built this room. That means somebody's able to take it apart."

"Don't think they left behind any tools."

The chief nodded. "But those jackasses didn't even frisk us." He produced a large, multipurpose folding knife from his pocket. "Let's look around for any screws in need of removin'."

They searched about for a moment then the chief blurted out, "Well lookee here, Michael. Someone was kind enough to leave the door hinge pins on the inside."

He took out the pocket knife and began to pry at one. It removed silently.

"Finally a break," said Michael.

No one responded to Joseph's knocking on the *Rebound* cabin door. The dinghy had an outboard engine with no ignition key. He'd take it in the belief Leo would understand. Joseph boarded the boat. *Finally some good luck,* he thought as he hefted the fuel tank and found it full, *enough for at least five hours.*

With *Vega* out of sight, Joseph motored out into the harbor. He believed it likely she would head toward the Strait of Juan de Fuca. If he took the southwest Mosquito Passage, he'd gain needed time. Fortunately, Leo stored a heavy flashlight to help access his crab pots in near darkness. Joseph found a laminated rainproof chart and appreciated the attention he'd paid to the Naval Academy piloting classes, though at the time wondered what use a Marine would have of being able to guide a ship down a channel.

He studied the chart that warned of kelp beds along his track. He'd watch out for them. Tangling his prop would delay him well beyond time gained through use of the Passage. A clear channel, well marked lay before him, and with the aid of Leo's flashlight, he could buoy hop his way to open water.

Now if only the Vega heads for the Strait, he thought. *If I'm wrong, I've missed her completely.*

Joseph settled down. Far too much had happened over the last half hour. He took a deep breath and reviewed the bidding. *Use all the think time you got,* counseled a gunny back at Basic in Quantico. *You'll be amazed at how much it lowers the mistake factor. And if you expect to stay alive in combat, the allowance for that is zero.*

Joseph reached the straight part of the channel where it widened enough to permit focus on other things. He decided to make a communications check and dialed up his dad's number on Doris's cell phone.

Before a full ring completed, he heard Liz's excited voice. "Hello! Joseph?"

"Yes," he replied and went on to explain his situation then asked if by any chance either saw which way the *Vega* turned after she cleared the channel.

"You certainly don't expect a couple of incompetent females to do that, now?"

He snapped, "C'mon, Liz! Haven't we got enough on our plate?"

He next heard Doris Baker's voice. "Are you okay, Joseph? Is the wind picking up or is that just my imagination?"

"Getting breezy," he replied.

She asked, "Life jacket?"

"Yeah, but there's a lot of reflective material on it. It'll make me easy to spot from the *Vega*."

"Put it on under your pullover, if that's a problem." Doris's voice became stern, "But keep that life jacket on, understand?"

"You got it, Mrs. B."

"So what is the plan, Joseph?"

"When I spot the *Vega,* I'll keep close and try to follow her. I'll keep in touch with you, and if I spot anything to warrant calling the Coast Guard, I'll let you know right away."

"Your boat fast enough?"

"Plenty," he replied. "Only problem is the waves kicking up, and this thing doesn't have a bilge pump. I got a bailing can, though. Just can't take on too much water, too fast. That would slow me down."

"You be careful, Joseph."

"I will, Mrs. B." *Whatever that means,* he thought.

Doris closed the phone and looked sternly at her daughter. She took a breath to say something harsh, but thought better of it. She wanted to be part of the solution, not the problem.

"What a mess," she fretted.

Liz looked at her mother. "I know you're worried, Mom. Guess you have a right to be." She withheld the urge to caution Doris about getting into such things and leave investigations to the authorities. "Toughest part is to sit here and do nothing except just wait."

Those who watch and wait also serve. The phrase ran through her mind, but Doris could not recall the author. "Maybe we got it all wrong. Frederick probably came back and might just have offered the guys a moonlight cruise. Who wouldn't enjoy an outing on the *Vega*? She's beautiful."

Her tone betrayed a lack of conviction. She knew also that Michael would have gone only if Doris joined him.

Liz knew her mom didn't believe a word of what she just said, but didn't argue. "Look, what harm is there in telling the Coast Guard exactly what we know? It can't hurt any."

Doris frowned, not wanting to commit herself too quickly. *Liz has a point,* she thought.

"We could tell them there's a crazy Marine Second Lieutenant bouncing around Haro Strait in a dinghy. Nothing so far, but he's an accident waiting to happen. If nothing else, they'd be alerted that there might be work for them out there."

"Good thought, Liz. But what if things start going back and forth on the Coast Guard radio circuit? I'm sure the *Vega* listens to that. How do we know that won't cause something bad to happen?"

"We don't, Mom. But the Coast Guard guys know about that. Let them decide."

"The problem is we have too little to tell them. All we know is the *Vega* has left port. We don't know for sure that Michael is aboard, much less if it isn't of his own free will."

"Okay, Mom. Let's walk over to Peter Bushnell's sailboat to see if they're there. If not, we might run into some people that saw something. But we can't just sit here and twiddle our thumbs."

Doris Baker came to grips with the fact her daughter showed signs of having begun *to put away childish things*. This feeling penetrated the great concern which now burdened her. What had become of the flighty ingénue with not a serious thought in her head?

"Sure. Let's go."

As they walked along the dock, Doris felt a comforting arm draped about her shoulder.

Joseph's heart sank. Nothing remotely resembling the *Vega* made its appearance in Haro Strait. Had he made a bad call? Did the *Vega* head northward toward Nanaimo, in Canadian waters?

Not having pencil, paper, calculator, or even dividers to measure distance on his chart, the entire operation had to be completed in his head. He wished he'd put more effort into the Academy Navigation course. He went over everything again. Approximate time of *Vega's* departure, distance she needed to run, and an estimated speed of ten knots through the water.

Damn, he thought. *No tide and current tables,* and this could make a significant difference in these waters. He had to go purely on his recollection of the last high tide. Thereafter, he recalled, it should reoccur every eleven hours. He comforted himself in the knowledge *Vega* bucked a max flood, making a late appearance likely. He knew it to be Lime Kiln light that winked at him from the south, but he checked his watch and confirmed the ten second interval.

To make matters worse, rising sea spilled into the dinghy, and he had to bail constantly. He had to maintain this heading into building seas until certain of the *Vega*'s disposition. He could not afford to lose distance to his objective. It would be tough to reach the palatial yacht and the smooth water in its wake. Joseph knew once these circumstances had been achieved he'd have speed advantage over his quarry.

Joseph, preoccupied with bailing, did not immediately spot the red port side light that emerged from the northern end of San Juan Island. The dinghy dry as he could get it, Joseph resumed his search in time to watch the craft make a turn to port, the masthead and range light coming close to alignment. It could be only the *Vega*, and he'd reached a position just about on her track. Instinctively, he slowed the dinghy to minimum speed and waves ceased to break over the unprotected bow.

The larger ship closed range. Before long, Joseph made out *Vega*'s unmistakable form.

Then he made a rookie mistake.

So elated he'd correctly reckoned her intended course and lucked upon a near perfect rendezvous, he completely forgot *Vega*'s huge bow wave. He struck it head on, and a violent pitch nearly tossed Joseph into the sea. The dinghy yawed to starboard, and the second bow wave dumped six inches of water into the dinghy.

With the tiny boat on the verge of swamping, he advanced the throttle to full and closed to find a calm spot in *Vega's* wake. Once there, he backed the throttle to maintain a distance of a hundred fifty yards astern and bailed out more sloshing water. He hoped no stern lookout would be posted on *Vega* and with Doris's advice, had covered the reflective surface of his life jacket with a pullover. Soaked, the jacket chilled Joseph to the bone, but pure adrenalin prevented him from noticing.

For an instant, life returned to normal. *Damn, I'm hungry,* he thought. Joseph basked in the pleasure of having taken a long shot and won, though more through luck than skill.

But an often heard saying by his adoptive father went, "Seems the harder I work, the luckier I get."

Joseph's hard work had apparently justified that philosophy.

Liz and Doris found Peter Bushnell's boat and adjacent docks empty. Everything at Roche had closed for the night. Where else could Michael be but on the *Vega*? And he would not have left without notifying her.

"We gotta notify the Coast Guard, Mom, and tell them what we know."

Doris replied, "You're right, honey. It's just ... I want to be sure it won't blow up in our faces."

"It won't, Mom. Look. How about I do the talking?"

Doris's silence spoke her agreement.

Back on the *Vietvet*, Doris got the Port Angeles Coast Guard station phone number from an emergency list prepared by the meticulous Jim Epsom. Liz dialed it.

A young female voice answered, "Port Angeles Coast Guard, Petty Officer Carter speaking. How may I help you?"

"Uh, we have a bit of a problem here. One of our friends has taken a small boat out into Haro Strait and we're worried about him."

"Are you in contact?"

Liz hesitated a second. *Better be straight up,* she thought. "He has a cell phone."

"Can you get him on it?"

"Yes, about half an hour ago," Liz replied.

"Did he say he was in any trouble?"

"No. But listen. This sounds crazy. There's reason to believe his father is being held on a big yacht against his will. The yacht's name is *Vega*, and he is trying to catch it."

"Do you have the *Vega*'s license number?"

"No."

"Can you contact your friend and get his position? Give me your number, and I'll have someone with more horsepower than me give you a call."

Liz read Michael's cell phone number then called Joseph.

When he answered, Liz declared, "General Baker speaking. Give me your position, Second Lieutenant Unger."

"That you, Liz? I don't have a compass, but I'd say six miles southwest of Lime Kiln light … trailing the *Vega* at a hundred fifty yards."

Liz noted the time. "Good. You hang in there Picky, and be careful."

Silence a moment then she demanded, "Did you hear me?"

"Yeah, Liz. If that's all, I'm signing off. Don't know how much battery is left in this thing."

Miguel Vargas stood on the *Vega*'s bridge in the posture of a man who did this before, and often. He raised binoculars and scanned the horizon ahead.

He ranted at Peter. "Kincaid and Porter had only suspected something was going on. Damn it, you brought them here and confirmed it for them. Look at the stupid mess we're in."

"Boss, I thought—"

Vargas cut him off. "You thought! You thought! Did your thoughts reveal you leave the four of us with two choices? We either finish off Kincaid and Porter or spend the rest of our lives in Walla Walla. Murder! That was never in the cards. And even if we finish them off, what does that woman of his know?"

Leo Walters, calmest of the lot spoke up. "Okay, what are all the options? C'mon. We're in a dangerous business. Risks come with the territory. Whatever Doris Baker knows, any case against us has to be proven in court. And the way we've covered our tracks, that won't be very damn easy to do."

Vargas asked, "Can the Baker woman be taken care of?"

Peter replied, "Coincident with the death of Kincaid … I don't think so."

Ben Schultz offered, "Can they be bought off? We got the bucks."

The remaining three would not dignify Ben's comments with a reply. He clearly did not have the keenest of minds.

Vargas said, "First things first. Let's make our rendezvous with the *Alcazar* and take care of that. Then see where we go from there."

Chapter 12

Chief Porter loosened the door hinge pins and set them back in place. It would not do for the door to fall off if opened when someone came by to check on them.

Michael asked, "How many do you think are aboard, Chief?"

"Dunno, but I figure it's a minimum crew."

"How many do they need to operate the yacht?"

"This boat's totally automatic. It can be run with one person as long as nothing craps out. Four is plenty enough to operate this tub."

"Vargas likely didn't bring anyone he doesn't need. Fewer witnesses, the better. What do you think he did with the household staff?"

The chief replied, "Hawke rents a nearby motel. Gives him a little privacy. Only Vargas and his wife live aboard. Look. We need a plan. One of us has got to slip outta here and look around. Hate to admit it, but you're younger and a helluva lot more mobile."

Chief Porter had a point. He'd overlooked Michael's limp but otherwise had it right.

"I'll slip out, get a nose count and see what I can see. Maybe someone's laid his weapon down and it's ours for the taking."

The chief nodded, though he thought that unlikely. "Try to locate some landmarks, and try to get a feel for the *Vega*'s position. That could be damn important."

"What if someone comes by to check while I'm gone?"

"I'll make a dummy from pillows and blankets and put it in the upper bunk. I'll tell whoever it is you're sleeping."

Neither thought much of the idea, but what other choice did they have? Michael wore navy blue slacks, his white shirt would stand out even in the dark.

The chief took off his black jacket. "Here. Wear this. It'll make you harder to spot."

"Thanks, Chief. When I get back, I'll give three raps at the bottom of the door."

Porter removed the pins then pressed his ear hard against the door. He heard nothing and gently pulled the door from its hinges, just enough to clear the door jamb. It provided ample slack to clear the lubricated deadbolt.

"Glad they keep everything in good shape."

Michael slipped out and again became a Recon Marine. Basic doctrine flowed automatically through his mind. *Secure the rear before advancing. Don't be taken from behind.* He figured everyone would be on the bridge. The chief had explained the yacht could be operated from there with no one stationed in other parts of the yacht.

Michael checked the engine room first then the other spaces. *Make sure everybody's up there.* Not good to be watching the bridge and have someone come up behind him.

The pair of Gray Marine diesel engines purred smoothly as they pushed *Vega* along through the rising seas, rolling slightly in the troughs. He'd guessed right and found the engine room unmanned. Flipping on the lights, he looked and considered the advantages to be taken.

He could decouple the engines and shut them down. That would make someone come down to investigate. Maybe he could ambush him and capture a weapon. Or perhaps trip out the generator and plunge the ship into darkness. *Bad idea. They likely have battery powered backup systems, and I'd gain nothing. Just wait, but keep thinking.*

Michael made his way forward, always alert for someplace to hide in case he heard someone. He checked along the row of cabins below deck, placed his ear to the door of each one and heard nothing. He moved forward through the lounge and paused beneath the ladder leading to the bridge.

Low voices could be heard from where he stood. Michael mounted the ladder and made out the forms of four men in the dimly lighted conning station. Closer now, he began to hear their conversation.

The unmistakable voice of Peter Bushnell spoke up. "I make us close to the rendezvous point, but no sign of the *Alcazar*. Maybe we should slow down."

Michael picked up on the name *Alcazar* and filed it away in memory.

Ben Schulz suggested, "Why not head west through the Strait and meet them sooner?"

Vargas explained, "Rough seas. It'll be tough enough to make the exchange here. Further out will be impossible."

Leo exclaimed, "Look! About ten miles west. A masthead light."

"Good," said Vargas. "That's probably it. He grasped a throttle in each hand and slowed the engines. "We'll let her come to us. Leo, check the signal lamp. Don't wait till we're in hailing distance to find out it doesn't work."

Leo picked up an Aldis lamp and tested it. "Bright light," he reported.

Michael's heart sank when he heard Vargas order, "Ben, you go below and check on our guests."

Joseph began to rapidly close on the *Vega* then backed off on the throttle. At a distance of thirty yards, he could read the name *Vega* in the halo of its stern light. *They've stopped. Something's likely about to happen. Better get on the phone.*

The excited voice of Liz answered, "Joseph?"

"Right, Liz."

"What's happening out there?"

"Not a lot," he replied. "The *Vega*'s slowed, so I figure she's where she wants to be. Listen. You got the time of my last position report?"

"Yeah. 11:30 p.m."

He looked at his watch. An hour had passed, and he could no longer see Lime Kiln Light and had run off Leo Walters' chart. A look skyward revealed the Big Dipper; its pointer stars showed the North Star to be directly behind him. He reckoned his speed over the last hour to be ten knots. "Look, Liz. Log the time and write that I'm ten miles south of my last position."

"You got it, Second Lieutenant Unger, Sir."

He shook off the remark. "The *Vega* runs slowly on a westerly heading to maintain steerageway."

"Steerageway? You exceeded my nautical knowledge with *westerly heading.*"

"Means she's moving just fast enough to keep her bow pointed in the direction she wants to go. One or two knots. Keep track of all the stuff I gave you and it'll be easy to figure out where we are."

"Why didn't you say that in the beginning, Picky?"

"Lost my head, I guess. Listen. The *Vega* is slowing down. I'll try to get close enough to climb aboard."

Liz shrieked at him, "Don't you dare, Picky! I'll tell Mom."

He next heard Doris's voice. "Joseph, what are you doing out there? Don't try to go aboard! Do you hear me?" She explained they had contacted the Coast Guard and didn't yet know how it would play out. "Best thing you can do is keep trailing them. If something happens, let us know and we'll pass it on. I'm not sure, but I think someone has to be in actual trouble before they can respond."

"Okay, Mrs. B., will let you know. Signing off now." *If something happens? Suppose 'something' is seeing the body of my dad tossed over the side.*

Joseph disregarded Doris's admonition and went ahead with his plan to board the *Vega*.

He located a hundred foot crab trap line and made it up to the bow of his dinghy. He would come to *Vega's* stern and toss a short line over a cleat on the stern platform. He'd secure the engine, make up the long line to the cleat, leap aboard, and release the short one, leaving the dinghy to trail a hundred feet behind.

His plan worked perfectly.

Chilled to the bone, he resisted his first instinct to find a place to get warm. He lay shivering on the platform and forced his mind to go over what little he knew of the *Vega*'s layout— based only on the social he had attended their first night at Roche. He'd simply feel his way about. After a time, he peeked carefully over the transom and saw or heard no one. He climbed up, opened the door to the lounge and entered.

The heat overcame his body chill like a warm blanket. He found a duct and stood before it to warm his numbed hands. *Wow, this feels good.*

Next, Joseph made his way forward through the darkened compartment. The bright stern light had diminished his night vision, still not fully recovered. Faint voices floated down to him from the bridge above and he began to climb the ladder with caution. Without warning, a powerful arm reached about his neck and a massive hand covered his mouth to prevent him from making a sound.

"Always cover your rear, Lieutenant Unger," whispered the voice of his father.

Ben Schulz stood before the cabin door to the compartment he believed to contain the chief and Michael. Pistol drawn, he gave the door a single rap. "Kincaid, Porter. You in there?"

"Who wants to know?" the chief demanded.

"Never mind. I hear you, Porter. Where's your friend?"

"Sleeping. Exactly what I'll be doing in a few minutes."

"You sure about that?"

Ben wished no confrontation, and it showed in his voice.

The chief picked up on it. "Come in and see for yourself."

"Never mind," said Ben. "You just better be telling me the truth."

He backed away from the door and returned to the bridge.

Michael pulled his son behind the lounge bar and explained the situation. "Either Ben Schultz will return quietly to the bridge or in a few moments, all hell's going to break loose."

They had not long to wait. Ben Schultz walked silently by them and made his way up the ladder to the bridge.

"Good," said Michael, "whatever the chief did, worked."

"Okay, Dad. Let's go get him. It'll be a bit cozy, but the three of us can make a landfall in the dinghy."

They returned to the cabin, and after Michael gave the prearranged signal, the door cracked then swung open.

The chief exclaimed, "Get in here, quick, Michael!"

"We got a break, Chief. Look who's here."

"Where did you come from?"

Joseph explained and said he could evacuate them in the dinghy.

The chief urged, "We better get a move on, then. Ben Schultz was just here checking on us."

Michael hesitated. He considered what Vargas and his crew might be about to do and wondered if it needed to be witnessed. *But right now, we got plenty enough to call in the Coast Guard, and Joseph had the foresight to bring along Doris's cell phone. The chief was right. Time to bail out.*

Porter removed the hinge pins and had almost pushed the door open when he heard the sound of footsteps. The chief stopped, and all froze in their tracks. Someone moved aft, in the direction of the dinghy.

When the footsteps faded, Michael whispered, "If they spot our ride, we're dead meat."

Stress filled moments filed by like a procession of tired snails. Salvation had passed close but seemed now on the verge of evading them.

Michael whispered, "Damn the luck."

All ears strained to hear the alarm given. Nothing. In a few moments, the footsteps retraced their way back from where they had come, the slow rhythm giving no indication the dinghy had been discovered.

"Probably a routine walk through the yacht," suggested the chief. "They're operating short-handed, so somebody's gotta take a look around now and then. Okay, let's get going."

He slipped the door out of the jamb, and the three exited, bringing with them what blankets they could find to stave off the chill they knew would be encountered.

"Hold it," the chief ordered. "Let's put the door back so it'll look like nothing's wrong if they come back."

Soon the three crouched on the sill behind, and Joseph began to pull in the hundred feet of line to the dinghy.

The feeling of elation dissolved as they heard the approaching voice of Peter Bushnell say, "Right back here, Miguel. I'll show you what I found."

They arrived at the fantail and caught sight of the would-be escapees.

"Well," snarled Vargas. "Looks like they don't appreciate our hospitality."

Both men drew their pistols and leveled them at the threesome on the platform.

"Hands up, where we can see them," Bushnell ordered.

The three complied.

Michael countered, "Listen, the jig is up for you guys. Too many of us are involved now and the Coast Guard knows your position. A cutter is probably en route right now."

"Just get your asses up here and back into your cage," ordered Bushnell. Then pointing toward Joseph he demanded, "Where the hell did you come from?"

"In the dinghy, you idiot," snapped Vargas. He shook his head to emphasize his displeasure with Peter. "Do you think you possibly can hold them here while I get the others?"

Bushnell smarted at the remark. "Yeah, Boss."

"Good. I'll bring some duct tape. This time, we fasten those busy hands behind their backs."

Vargas disappeared.

"Look, Bushnell," declared Michael, "face up to the facts. Joseph has a cell phone, and people ashore know where you are, and you're holding us against our will. Don't make matters worse for yourselves."

"Shut up! We'll do the talking now. And you! Give me that damn cell phone."

Joseph complied.

The chief's anger exploded at the man who had feigned friendship for so many years. "Go to hell, Peter!"

He drew a breath to say more, but didn't. This would best wait for another time.

Vargas returned with the others with weapons drawn. He handed a fresh roll of duct tape to Leo Walters.

"Tape their hands behind them. This time individual cabins for each. We don't want any more of their damned cooperative thinking. Afterward, meet me on the bridge."

Almost in unison, they all replied, "Yeah boss."

Michael looked at his son. Glances exchanged between them needed no words. Michael's thoughts went to the Ungers, his son's diligent adoptive parents. Joseph would not be in this situation if Michael had not made the attempt to find him.

Miguel Vargas looked grimly from face to face. "No need to tell you the seriousness of our situation. I believe our choices are limited to two."

"What's that, Boss?"

Ben Shultz's voice revealed a total lack of confidence. He'd surrendered and could no longer think for himself. Vargas would have to do that for him.

Leo asked, "Two choices? What?"

"If we do nothing, its thirty years apiece at Walla Walla. Kidnapping, for openers and it won't take long for the authorities to dope out the rest."

"You said two, Miguel," retorted Peter.

"We can send this tub to the bottom and disappear into Canada. From there, it's every man for himself."

Leo, Ben and Peter exchanged astonished glances.

Peter spoke, "Have you thought this through, Miguel?"

"Many times. Did you believe for a moment something like this could never happen?"

The three remained silent.

"Of course you didn't. None of you have an original thought in your head. Listen carefully. I have several large explosive charges hidden in the bilges, ready for activation. Five minute timers. When they go, the *Vega* will head to the bottom in a matter of minutes. Sixty fathoms, which means it can be reached if anyone takes the trouble to find it. Better to take it out in the Pacific, but we don't have the time. After we blow her, the four of us will be off in one of the Zodiacs. We'll make it to Canada, scuttle the boat far enough off shore, and swim to the beach."

Appearing on the verge of a nervous breakdown, Ben asked, "Then what?"

"Half a million in cash for each of us, conveniently stashed in waterproof sacks. That ought to offset any situation that might be encountered. Money is the universal persuader."

Leo added, "I guess there'll be questions, but no one can prove we didn't go down with the *Vega*."

"Ah, Leo. You amaze me. How come I didn't stumble upon such logic?"

Miguel's sarcasm seared through all except Ben, who asked, "But what of our families?"

Miguel said through a cynical voice, "Ah yes. Wouldn't it be better to shame them with the disgust of our deeds? They could visit us in prison. And Ben. Why with time off for good behavior, you could be reunited ... say when you're ninety-five."

The other two shared Ben's concern, but not quite so devastated by the prospects. They listened and accepted Miguel's logic. It had been a profitable ride for a considerable time, now. Time to pay the piper.

Peter asked, "So what do we do with the chief, Kincaid and the boy?"

"Witnesses destroy any plausible theory that we went down with the *Vega*."

The realization of what Miguel implied struck all three in the gut.

Ben, almost hysterical, screamed, "We can't just murder them!"

Miguel replied calmly, "Then your vote is for life at Walla Walla. What say the rest of you?"

"Your plan," said Peter.

"Me too," added Leo.

"And you, Ben?"

He could only offer a nod.

"Good," said Miguel. "Assemble our guests in the lounge. I have a sense that none of you have the stomach for this, so I'll see to it myself. But I insist you be present. One of you come back to the bridge, and let me know when all is in readiness. This will provide, shall we say, a certain measure of mutual security for the future? My finger will be on the trigger but with the assent of each of you."

The three nodded and went off to collect the chief, Michael and Joseph.

Vargas thought of quite a different plan. He opened a locker, removed a Micro-Uzi submachine gun and installed a fully loaded magazine.

Then in his mind, he went over his real plan. *It's equally easy to gun down six as three. My half-assed accomplices first, as their hands are free. What a pleasure it will be to dispatch that wimp, Shultz. The world needs to be rid of his kind. All greed and no stomach. Then my erstwhile guests. Nothing against them except they'd thwart my plan. The lad, Joseph. Such a fine young man, but there are plenty others. And me. Still enough darkness left to take a Zodiac back to Roche. Sink it a short distance off shore, then swim to the beach. From there, a short walk to the motel, where I shall resume the role of humble, meek, faithful servant, Miguel Vargas, completely befuddled by the news which inevitably will break in the morning. Upon realization of the Vega's loss, total remorse. Next, just a question of time before Frederick is taken care of, either by manipulating local authorities, or some other means. Then, the Thomas Hawke legacy, which has me, the good and faithful servant, second in line for that fortune. The days ahead are far better than I might ever have imagined.*

The quavering voice of Peter Bushnell interrupted Miguel's reflections. "Everybody's assembled in the lounge, Boss."

Chapter 13

An irate Vargas demanded, "Where the hell's Schultz?"

The chief, Joseph and Michael stood together in the lounge, wrists duct taped behind them. The sight of Miguel Vargas's Uzi sub-machine gun did not reassure them.

"He has no stomach for this," said Peter. "He'll join us afterward."

Each of the intended victims understood the significance of Peter's *afterward*. Even during the darkest days of Vietnam, Michael had never experienced a feeling of such total futility. Like rats in a trap they awaited their ultimate fate, helpless to do anything about it. Michael's mind raced in pursuit of a solution, but could think only of a verbal plea for their lives, not likely to be successful with the heartless Miguel Vargas.

"Go get him," snarled Miguel, "bring the sniveling bastard up here. We all watch."

Leo and Peter exchanged fretful glances.

"I'll get him," said Peter.

Shortly, Ben Schultz appeared, a man devastated beyond comprehension. "Please, Miguel. Don't make me watch this."

Vargas exclaimed, "You yellow coward!"

Schultz's wavering voice approached being indiscernible. "We don't have to do this, Boss. Why can't we just get in the boat and go?"

Michael quickly studied the faces of Peter and Leo that showed them in complete agreement with Ben.

Vargas responded in a dispassionate voice. "You want jail for the rest of our lives."

A metallic snap signaled the Uzi safety being disabled.

"No, dammit!" Ben reached back and drew from some unknown resolve.

"No? A gutless pig tells me no?"

Then, wonder of wonders. Ben stepped forward and positioned himself between Vargas and his intended victims.

"No! Murder was never in the deal, and you'll not make me a party to it."

"Perhaps you'd like to join our friends, then?" Vargas raised the Uzi. "Stand aside or you will."

He had no second thoughts over killing Schultz, part of his plan anyway. *A bit sooner won't hurt.*

"I said no, dammit!"

Ben Schultz drew his automatic and leveled it at Vargas. The two men faced off for an instant.

Beneath an impassive snarl, Vargas pressed his trigger first. In one second, twenty-one nine millimeter bullets entered Ben Schultz's torso, killing him instantly. But not before a death throe spasm caused his gun hand to contract, discharging his pistol and sending a huge forty-five caliber copper jacket bullet through the evil heart of Miguel Vargas. Both men lay dead on the *Vega* lounge floor.

One of the bullets passed through Ben Schultz and struck Joseph in the right arm, whirling him about and onto the floor.

Michael yelled out, agony clear in his voice. "Joseph!"

"I'm okay, Dad."

Michael looked at Peter Bushnell and with a tone of anger said, "Get this damn stuff off my wrists so I can look after my boy."

Neither Walters nor Bushnell had drawn their weapons.

"Turn around," said Peter, and he pulled the duct tape from Michael's wrists.

"Have either of you got a knife?"

Michael remembered the one in the chief's pocket which had been used to pry hinge pins from their cabin door. He removed it, severed the duct tape bonds of his son's wrists then cut through the sleeve of his pullover.

"Turn around, Chief, and I'll get you."

After releasing Porter, Michael refocused attention on his son and found a clean entry wound below Joseph's shoulder.

The bullet's energy had dissipated during its passage through Ben Schultz's torso, so remained embedded in Joseph's arm. Infection would pose the greatest risk. Luckily, the bullet appeared to have missed his humerus bone.

"Get me a first aid kit," Michael instructed Leo Walters, who complied immediately.

Both Walters and Bushnell signaled with body language that the crisis had passed. There'd be no further trouble from them.

Joseph said, "We better contact Mrs. B. and Liz. They gotta be worried sick by now."

Michael nodded. "We'll just let them know everything's under control." He doubted Doris's intuition would buy it. "And we need to get the Coast Guard out here. Chief, check the GPS for a position."

"Should we use the radio, Dad? Not sure how much longer the cell battery will hold out."

It pleased Michael to see his son alert and articulate. "We better low-key it. There's a ship, the *Alcazar*, likely not far away. Overheard Vargas say it was to rendezvous with the *Vega*. It might not be good if they're monitoring the Coast Guard frequency and become alerted."

The chief returned. "Forty eight-twenty north, one twenty three-ten west. Well inside U.S. waters, so no jurisdiction problems." He handed Michael a scrap of paper. "Here. I wrote it down."

Leo Walters returned with a first aid kit. Michael ordered, "Clean up Joseph's wound, Chief." Turning to Walters and Bushnell, he continued, "You two go find some blankets, and cover Vargas and Schultz."

The two moved out immediately. Michael made it obvious he had taken charge. Neither Walters nor Bushnell had surrendered their firearms, but kept them tucked in their belts. Michael handed the Micro-Uzi to Chief Porter and tucked the late Ben Schultz's forty-five into his own belt.

Just like old times.

Doris answered, surprised to hear Michael's voice. "That Joseph! He did go aboard, after I distinctly told him not to."

"He's ornery, like his old man."

"Is he hurt, Michael? He is. I can hear it in your voice."

"A little roughed up, but okay. He's a Marine." *That woman is uncanny.*

"You better not be lying to me, Michael."

Michael gritted his teeth. "Call the Coast Guard, Doris. Tell them there's a situation that requires immediate attention. Also, be on the lookout for a foreign ship, the *Alcazar*. Evidence here is some major laws are being broken. Mention kidnapping, but say everything is settled down and the good guys are in control. There is no danger in approaching us."

He gave her the *Vega*'s position.

"But you and Joseph are okay? Not in any danger?"

"No, Doris. And it's a good thing Joseph came aboard. You and I wouldn't be having this conversation if he hadn't."

"If he's okay, let me talk to him."

"Look, Sweetie, we gotta hang up. This battery won't last forever, and it's all we got to stay in touch. Okay?"

"Okay," she said. *Sweetie. Finally a pet name. I wouldn't say a fit for classic English Literature, but at least a start.*

Doris heard the phone ring several times at Port Angeles Coast Guard, before a man answered and identified himself as Lieutenant Baldwin.

"Yes, Ma'am, I was just about to call you. I understand you have a situation. Can you give me any more information?"

Doris recited everything passed to her since her earlier conversation with Petty Officer Crawford."

"Well that's plenty enough for us to act on. We have a cutter ready to go. Based on your info, we should make an intercept within the hour," said Lieutenant Baldwin.

"Sir." Doris's voice resonated with an uncharacteristic quaver. "The people onboard said problems might grow out of calling them on the Coast Guard circuit. Another ship, the

Alcazar, is involved, and should not be alerted. Here, let me give you the cell phone number."

"Yes, Ma'am. We'll contact them by cell phone, if that's what you wish."

"Good. Do you have medical personnel aboard the cutter?"

"No, Ma'am. Is there a problem?"

"Call it woman's intuition, but I believe there is. I suspect they may be sparing us the details."

"I'll call them. In the meantime, we'll summon a doctor to the cutter immediately. We have one on call, so it won't take long."

"Thank you so much, Lieutenant Baldwin."

"Ma'am. I expect the people aboard the *Vega* are important to you. We'll proceed with all dispatch."

"Thank you, Lieutenant," Doris replied. "Sir?"

"Yes, Ma'am."

"Could you hurry?"

"We sure will."

Doris hung up, and turned to Liz. "Now comes fun time: waiting. I guess that's what we women do best."

"I don't see how anybody in their right mind could be a Marine, Mom. Those guys just attract trouble."

"Hello. Kincaid speaking."

"Lieutenant Baldwin from Port Angeles Coast Guard, sir. Can you report your situation, please?"

Michael summarized the *Vega*'s circumstances and gave their position.

"Is the injured man stable? Do we need a helo evacuation?" Baldwin asked.

"He's standing right here beside me and seems okay. But I expect there'll be a sore arm tomorrow."

"We have a doctor aboard and are heading in your direction. Can you take a course for Port Angeles, please? I'm afraid we'll have to impound the yacht based on all that's happened. The police will need a real good look."

"We're already heading your way at seven knots." Michael considered the problem of Doris and Liz still at Roche but knew it would have to keep for a later time. "There is another vessel likely involved in this incident. All I have is the name, *Alcazar.*"

"We'll check her out. But you guys are a bird in the hand and get priority."

"Thank you," Michael replied.

Peter and Leo returned with blankets to cover the bodies of Schultz and Vargas. Michael noticed that the chief avoided contact with his former friend and had stationed himself where he could do the most good: on the bridge.

"We should search Vargas," said Peter. "He's got four waterproof packages of cash on him."

Peter went on with obvious embarrassment to explain their thwarted plan.

"You won't find a dime on him," Michael replied. "Are you stupid enough to believe Vargas planned for the three of you to end up anywhere but at the bottom of the Strait? Use your head, man. He had no further need for you, and Vargas's sense of loyalty is a few notches below a rattlesnake's."

Michael's remark angered Peter. "We'll just see about that."

He searched Vargas's corpse and found nothing.

"That bastard was going to gun you guys down and make it back to Roche. No one had to know he was even out here."

"Damn him," seethed Walters. "I hope he rots in hell."

Michael explained to both that the Coast Guard would soon be boarding, and it would be a good thing for them to turn over their weapons. "You don't want to be armed when they get here."

Leo complied instantly, but Peter hesitated, searching for an alternative, but found none. Reluctantly, he then handed over his weapon to Michael.

Late Monday afternoon, Doris met Michael at the Olympic Medical Center in Port Angeles. She and Liz had flown down from San Juan Island via the local air service.

She greeted him, first with a hug then an admonition, "Don't you ever do anything like that again. We both were worried sick."

"Not if I can help it. It was not my idea of a lotta fun."

"So you say. Is Joseph okay? What happened out there?"

He summarized the shooting event. "Nothing serious. Got a bullet stuck in his right shoulder."

"That's what you call not serious?"

"No, not actually. The bullet was fairly well spent before it hit him. Problem is it didn't pass through, so they'll have to dig it out. That'll hurt a lot more than when he got it."

"Oh. Poor Joseph."

"He's a tough kid."

Doris thought, *Like father, like son,* but didn't say it.

He asked, "Where's Liz?"

"Parking the car. She'll be right in. By the way, she's furious with Joseph for being so reckless."

Michael could see why, but only said, "That's something they'll have to work out."

Doris agreed, but didn't say so. "Listen, you tell me everything that happened out there, and don't spare any details."

Michael took her from the initial conversation with the chief and Bushnell of the previous evening to the present.

"I have a problem. Why were all the guilty parties so anxious for us to get started on the case?"

"It's simple, actually. Vargas must have figured Frederick developed a feel for what went on. He likely believed my overstated success with the Blackwood case earned me enough credibility with law enforcement to make it a factor. And if I found new evidence to implicate Frederick, it would get him out of the way. Vargas might have succeeded, but when Peter Bushnell got wind of what passed between the chief and me on what he observed at the Hawke farm, everything changed.

Peter overreacted when he took us to Vargas, and that turned everything around."

"And everyone seemed so eager to help. They were just fishing us in?"

"You got it."

"Even Ben Schultz's list?"

"Likely it was composed by Vargas. He had me completely fooled. Played the role of humble servant to the hilt. When I first encountered his personality reversal, it just about floored me."

Doris said, "I was astounded too when I learned Miguel was the *heavy*. And poor Ceely Schultz. Do you think she was implicated? And what of Isabel Vargas? Her too? I'd find that hard to believe."

"We'll never know, though I suspect the police will work both over pretty hard. Thing that blows me away ... Thomas Hawke's death triggered our whole involvement in this and turns out he wasn't murdered after all."

Doris shook her head. "Well, that's the last of this kind of thing for us, right Harry Steele?"

"Right as rain, Agatha Christie."

At that point, Liz walked in. The set of her chin signaled Michael would have to go through the whole story again. He looked at Doris through an expression that pleaded for help.

She simply shrugged and shook her head.

After inquiring about Joseph, Liz said to Michael in an irritated voice, "Well, begin at the beginning and don't skip a single thing."

Epilogue

Wednesday morning, Michael sat in his study, a warm shaft of sunlight shining through the window and onto his desk. A full cup of coffee sat on a coaster, given to him by Doris, who while during a recent visit, noticed coffee cup circles all over his desktop. He reread the front page on the Peninsula Daily News edition spread out before him. The lead article read:

Two Arraigned from Yacht Vega on White Slavery Charges

Leo Walters of Port Ludlow, and Peter Bushnell of Eastern Washington, are being held for arraignment in Clallam County Courthouse today on charges of white slavery, kidnapping, and complicity in attempted murder. Walters and Bushnell were implicated in an operation to illegally import infants for adoption and women for prostitution.

The Yacht *Vega*, property of Frederick Hawke of Seattle and Eastern Washington, was instrument in these alleged crimes, and is impounded at the U.S. Coast Guard Station, Port Angeles. A preliminary investigation reveals no complicity by Hawke, who was unavailable for comment during attempts by the News to contact him by phone.

Events came to a head Sunday evening when a shooting aboard the *Vega* took the lives of Miguel Vargas, a longtime employee of Hawke, and Benjamin Schultz of Eastern Washington. Both of the dead were complicit in the allegations against Walters and Bushnell. The *Vega* was north of Port Angeles in the Strait, allegedly en route to a rendezvous for the transfer of illegals from an unknown vessel, currently being sought by the Coast Guard and Immigration Service.

Kidnapping victims were Michael Kincaid, Professor at the University of Washington, Port Angeles Campus, his son, 2nd Lieutenant Joseph Unger, a recent graduate of the U.S. Naval Academy, and Stanley Porter of Eastern Washington. Kincaid and Porter are retired, respectively from the U.S. Marine Corps and the U.S. Navy. Porter served with distinction as a submariner in World War II.

Lieutenant Unger was wounded during the encounter, but released from the Olympic Medical Center here on Tuesday morning. He is currently assigned to the Marine Corps base at Camp Pendleton, CA. According to several accounts, the Lieutenant's heroic actions saved the lives of his father and Stanley Porter.

Michael heard sounds from the guest bedroom as Joseph readied himself for a ride to the airport for the trip to Camp Pendleton. Against doctor's orders, he frequently pulled his arm from the sling to perform the involved chores.

A tough case, thought Michael. *Wonder who he gets that from?* "Better get a move on, Joseph. We gotta stop off and say good-bye to Doris and Liz.

"Ready, Dad."

Joseph emerged from the guest room in summer khakis, with a valise in his hand.

Well, at least he's carrying it in his good hand. Admiration for his son showed on his face. Joseph tossed his bag in the trunk and they climbed into Michael's restored 1970 Ford Falcon.

"You can get Mrs. B. in this, Dad? Sure doesn't look like her kind of ride."

Michael smiled. "Well, there have been suggestions. By the way, morning papers say you're a hero."

"Dad, I was never so scared in my life. I always thought Marines weren't supposed to get that way."

"Son. If you're not scared, that's when you've really got to worry. Fear makes an honest man out of you. Its absence makes you reckless."

"We never talked about Nam, Dad. Maybe we should."

"Sure, Joseph. We'll do that. But one thing you should know right now, you handled yourself exceptionally well in a combat situation. That will hold you in good stead for whatever lies ahead."

"Thanks, Dad."

They remained silent for the final minutes of their drive to Doris's apartment. She greeted them at the door.

"Oh, Joseph. Your arm!" She reached out for him but restrained herself because he appeared so fragile—her mothering instincts obvious.

He tried to shake it off. "Stings a little, but I think I'll pull through." He looked past Doris to Liz. *Really struck out with her,* he thought. "Liz, Guess you head back to the U soon."

"Tomorrow," she replied.

"Plan to freeload with your mom?"

Joseph wanted to keep the conversation light.

"Isn't that a kid's job? Freeload on their parents?"

"Just got through doing that with Dad, gotta keep the faith."

Michael warned, "Sorry, but we've got to cut this short. Plane's on schedule, and I doubt they'll wait for us.

Joseph extended his left hand to Liz. "Guess this will have to do. Had a really great time, Liz. Terrific meeting you."

Michael and Doris looked on, not knowing what to expect.

"You too, Joseph. Good luck with the training."

"Thanks." Joseph then turned to Doris. "Had a wonderful time, Mrs. B."

Doris gave him a hug, taking care to avoid his shoulder. "Come back soon, but not so much adventure next time."

"Will see what I can do, and Mrs. B?"

"Yes, Joseph?"

"For the record, I don't know which I like best. Dad's good taste or his eye for beautiful women."

Bowled over, but only for an instant, Doris thought, *Now there's a young man who knows what to say to a woman. Must've got it from his adoptive father.* "Thank you, Joseph. You be careful down there. I know I told you that before. You didn't listen and see what happened. This time I mean it, hear?"

"Hear." He smiled at her then walked to the Falcon.

Liz raced by Doris and Michael like a shot from a gun. "Damn you, Picky, get back here."

Joseph stopped and turned to face Liz.

She shouted, "You just don't walk into my life, and then … trot out like it's just another day."

He replied, "But I thought—"

She cut him off, threw her arms around his neck and held him close. "Can't you ever stand still and not say anything?"

Michael turned to Doris and said, "Any chance they'll beat us to the altar?"

"Michael Kincaid! Is that a proposal?"

"Of course."

"What's a poor girl to do but crumble under such romantic words?"

"I can take that as a *yes*?"

"But if a hug and a kiss don't go with your sorry excuse for a proposal, I'll change my mind."

"Can't have that now, can we?" They embraced. "How about we catch a plane up to Roche? A few sunny days left, and the *Vietvet*'s still there. We gotta bring it back, you know. That romantic enough?"

"Getting close," Doris said. "Keep working at it, and you might even get to sleep in the main bunkroom."

Joseph returned Liz's hug as best he could with one arm. "Can I ask just one thing?"

"Yes, I'll drive you to the damn airport," she replied. Liz had clearly inherited her mom's uncanny intuition.

About the Author

 Beginning with *Missing Person*, D.M. Ulmer continued the stories writing as the sole author of the second in this Caper Series, *The Roche Harbor Caper*. His newest addition to this series, *The Long Beach Caper*, is scheduled for a Summer 2010 release.

D.M. Ulmer is a history buff and writes for a variety of periodicals. He lives with his wife, Carol, in Redmond, Washington. Visit his website: DMUlmer.com

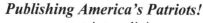
Silent Battleground by D.M. Ulmer

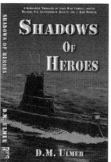

The Cold War did go hot when the Soviet Union attacked the U.S. Navy coastal installations and all but destroyed the American surface fleet. Ulmer moves the reader through tense combat events with skill and expertise using his 32 years of experience as a professional submariner to make this a page-turner complete with intrigue and speculation. Reviewers are touting this naval-action thriller about submarine warfare as the next *Hunt for Red October*.

Shadows of Heroes by D.M. Ulmer

January 1949, early in the undeclared *Cold War*, the U.S. diesel-electric submarine *Kokanee* has illegally penetrated deep into Soviet Union waters of the White Sea and is detected by a pair of Russian destroyers. Depth charges fall on *Kokanee* and seem on the verge of tearing the besieged ship apart. A vindictive Russian captain is determined to eradicate the Americans.

Count the Ways by D.M. Ulmer

A grand romance in the classic sense. A love between a Naval Academy midshipman and an Iowa farm girl, a Korean War-era tragedy, and the search by a grandson for the mystery surrounding his grandparents' love story.